Poul Anderson, recently voted the most popular author of science fiction, has created the largest and longest future-history series in the s-f field. In the tradition of Robert A. Heinlein's classic stories, Anderson chronicles the future spread of mankind throughout the galaxy, featuring such famous characters as Dominic Flandry, David Falkayn and Nicholas Van Rijn, the hero of *Trader To The Stars*. The voyages of Van Rijn, the wily trader, take place against the background of a coalescing galactic empire in an heroic age of pioneering independence.

''The world's great age begins anew....''

By the Same Author

STAR PRINCE CHARLIE
with Gordon Dickson

HOWARD AND BEYOND

TRADER
TO THE STARS

POUL ANDERSON

A BERKLEY MEDALLION BOOK
published by
BERKLEY PUBLISHING CORPORATION

To Gordon Dickson

Published by arrangement with Doubleday & Company

Doubleday & Company
Garden City, New York

SBN 425-03199-3

BERKLEY MEDALLION BOOKS are published by
Berkley Publishing Corporation
200 Madison Avenue
New York, N. Y. 10016

BERKLEY MEDALLION BOOK® TM 757,375

Printed in the United States of America

Berkley Medallion Edition, August 1976

Most of this book has appeared in *Astounding
Science Fiction*, copyright ©1956 by Street &
Smith Publications, Inc., and in *Analog Science
Fact—Science Fiction*, copyright ©1961, 1963,
1964 by The Condé Nast Publications, Inc. *Margin
of Profit*, quoted, has also appeared in *Un—Man
and Other Novellas*, copyright ©1962
by Ace Books, Inc.

"The world's great age begins anew . . ."

As it has before, and will again. The comings and goings of man have their seasons.

They are no more mysterious than the annual cycle of the planet, and no less. Because today we are sailing out among the stars, we are more akin to Europeans over-running America or Greeks colonizing the Mediterranean littoral than to our ancestors of only a few generations ago. We, too, are discoverers, pioneers, traders, missionaries, composers of epic and saga. Our people have grown bolder than their fathers, ambitious, individualistic; on the darker side, greed, callousness, disregard for the morrow, violence, often outright banditry have returned. Such is the nature of societies possessed of, and by, a frontier.

Yet no springtime is identical with the last. Technic civilization is not Classical or Western; and as it spreads ever more thinly across ever less imaginable reaches of space—as its outposts and its heartland learn, for good or ill, that which ever larger numbers of nonhuman peoples have to teach: it is changing in ways unpredictable. Already we live in a world that no Earthbound man could really have comprehended.

He might, for instance, have seen an analogy between the Polesotechnic League and the mercantile guilds of medieval Europe. But on closer examination he would find that here is something new, descended indeed from concepts of the Terrestrial past but with mutation and miscegenation in its bloodlines.

We cannot foretell what will come of it. We do not know where we are going. Nor do most of us care. For us it is enough that we are on our way.

—Le Matelot

HIDING PLACE

Captain Bahadur Torrance received the news as befitted a Lodgemaster in the Federated Brotherhood of Spacemen. He heard it out, interrupting only with a few knowledgeable questions. At the end, he said calmly, "Well done, Freeman Yamamura. Please keep this to yourself till further notice. I'll think about what's to be done. Carry on." But when the engineer officer had left the cabin—the news had not been the sort you tell on the intercom—he poured himself a triple whiskey, sat down, and stared emptily at the viewscreen.

He had traveled far, seen much, and been well rewarded. However, promotion being swift in his difficult line of work, he was still too young not to feel cold at hearing his death sentence.

The screen showed such a multitude of stars, hard and winter-brilliant, that only an astronaut could recognize individuals. Torrance sought past the Milky Way until he identified Polaris. Then Valhalla would lie so-and-so many degrees away, in *that* direction. Not that he could see a type-G sun at this distance, without optical instruments more powerful than any aboard the *Hebe G.B.* But he found a certain comfort in knowing his eyes were sighted toward the nearest League base (houses, ships, humans, nestled in a green valley on Freya) in this almost uncharted section of our galactic arm. Especially when he didn't expect to land there, ever again.

The ship hummed around him, pulsing in and out of fourspace with a quasi-speed that left light far behind and yet was still too slow to save him.

Well . . . it became the captain to think first of the others. Torrance sighed and stood up. He spent a moment checking his appearance; morale was important, never more so than now. Rather than the usual gray coverall of shipboard, he preferred full uniform: blue tunic, white cape and culottes, gold braid. As a citizen of Ramanujan planet, he kept a turban on his dark aquiline head, pinned with the Ship-and-Sunburst of the Polesotechnic League.

He went down a passageway to the owner's suite. The steward was just leaving, a tray in his hand. Torrance signaled the door to remain open, clicked his heels and bowed. "I pray pardon for the interruption, sir," he said. "May I speak privately with you? Urgent."

Nicholas van Rijn hoisted the two-liter tankard which had been brought him. His several chins quivered under the stiff goatee; the noise of his gulping filled the room, from the desk littered with papers to the Huy Brasealian jewel-tapestry hung on the opposite bulkhead. Something by Mozart lilted out of a taper. Blond, big-eyed, and thoroughly three-dimensional, Jeri Kofoed curled on a couch, within easy reach of him where he sprawled in his lounger. Torrance, who was married but had been away from home for some time, forced his gaze back to the merchant.

"Ahhh!" Van Rijn banged the empty mug down on a table and wiped foam from his mustaches. "Pox and pestilence, but the first beer of the day is good! Something with it is so quite cool and—um—by damn, what word do I want?" He thumped his sloping forehead with one hairy fist. "I get more absent in the mind every week. Ah, Torrance, when you are too a poor old lonely fat man with all powers failing him, you will look back and remember me and wish you was more good to me. But then is too late." He sighed like a minor tornado and scratched the pelt on his chest. In the near tropic temperature at which he insisted on maintaining his quarters, he need wrap only a sarong about his huge body. "Well, what be-gobbled stupiding is it I must be dragged from my-all-too-much work to fix up for you, ha?"

His tone was genial. He had, in fact, been in a good mood ever since they escaped the Adderkops. (Who wouldn't be? For a mere space yacht, even an armed one with ultrapowered engines, to get away from three cruis-ers, was more than an accomplishment; it was very nearly a miracle. Van Rijn still kept four grateful candles burn-ing before his Martian sandroot statuette of St. Dismas.) True, he sometimes threw crockery at the steward when a drink arrived later than he wished, and he fired every-body aboard ship at least once a day. But that was normal.

Jeri Kofoed arched her brows. "Your first beer, Nicky?" she murmured. "Now really! Two hours ago—"

"*Ja,* but that was before midnight time. If not Green-wich midnight, then surely on some planet somewhere, *nie?* So is a new day." Van Rijn took his churchwarden off the table and began stuffing it. "Well, sit down, Cap-tain Torrance, make yourself to be comfortable and lend me your lighter. You look like a dynamited custard, boy. All you youngsters got no stamina. When I was a working spaceman, by Judas, we made solve all our own problems. These days, death and damnation, you come ask me how to wipe your noses! Nobody has any guts but me." He slapped his barrel belly. "So what is be-jingle-bang gone wrong now?"

Torrance wet his lips. "I'd rather speak to you alone, sir."

He saw the color leave Jeri's face. She was no coward. Frontier planets, even the pleasant ones like Freya, didn't breed that sort. She had come along on what she knew would be a hazardous trip because a chance like this—to get an in with the merchant prince of the Solar Spice & Liquors Company, which was one of the major forces within the whole Polesotechnic League—was too good for an opportunistic girl to refuse. She had kept her nerve during the fight and the subsequent escape, though death came very close. But they were still far from her planet, among unknown stars, with the enemy hunting them.

"So go in the bedroom," Van Rijn ordered her.

"Please," she whispered. "I'd be happier hearing the truth."

The small black eyes, set close to Van Rijn's hook nose, flared. "Foulness and fulminate!" he bellowed. "What is this poppies with cocking? When I say frog, by billy damn, you jump!"

She sprang to her feet, mutinous. Without rising, he slapped her on the appropriate spot. It sounded like a pistol going off. She gasped, choked back an indignant screech, and stamped into the inner suite. Van Rijn rang for the steward.

"More beer this calls for," he said to Torrence. "Well, don't stand there making bug's eyes! I got no time for fumblydiddles, even if you overpaid loafer do. I got to make revises of all price schedules on pepper and nutmeg for Freya before we get there. Satan and stenches! At least ten percent more that idiot of a factor could charge them, and not reduce volume of sales. I swear it! All good saints, hear me and help a poor old man saddled with oatmeal-brained squatpots for workers!"

Torrance curbed his temper with an effort. "Very well, sir. I just had a report from Yamamura. You know we took a near miss during the fight, which hulled us at the engine room. The converter didn't seem damaged, but after patching the hole, the gang's been checking to make sure. And it turns out that about half the circuitry for the infrashield generator was fused. We can't replace more than a fraction of it. If we continue to run at full quasi-speed, we'll burn out the whole converter in another fifty hours."

"Ah, s-s-so." Van Rijn grew serious. The snap of the lighter, as he touched it to his pipe, came startlingly loud. "No chance of stopping altogether to make fixings?

Once out of hyperdrive, we would be much too small a thing for the bestinkered aderkops to find. Hey?"

"No, sir. I said we haven't enough replacement parts. This is a yacht, not a warship."

"Hokay, we must continue in hyperdrive. How slow must we go, to make sure we come within calling distance of Freya before our engine burns out?"

"One-tenth of top speed. It'd take us six months."

"No, my captain friend, not so long. We never reach Valhalla star at all. The Adderkops find us first."

"I suppose so. We haven't got six months' stores aboard anyway." Torrance stared at the deck. "What occurs to me is, well, we could reach one of the nearby stars. There just barely might be a planet with an industrial civilization, whose people could eventually be taught to make the circuits we need. A habitable planet, at least— maybe . . ."

"*Nie!*" Van Rijn shook his head till the greasy black ringlets swirled about his shoulders. "All us men and one woman, for life on some garbagey rock where they have not even wine grapes? I'll take an Adderkop shell and go out like a gentleman, by damn!" The steward appeared. "Where you been snoozing? Beer, with God's curses on you! I need to make thinks! How you expect I can think with a mouth like a desert in midsummer?"

Torrance chose his words carefully. Van Rijn would have to be reminded that the captain, in space, was the final boss. And yet the old devil must not be antagonized, for he had a record of squirming between the horns of dilemmas. "I'm open to suggestions, sir, but I can't take the responsibility of courting enemy attack."

Van Rijn rose and lumbered about the cabin, fuming obscenities and volcanic blue clouds. As he passed the shelf where St. Dismas stood, he pinched the candles out in a marked manner. That seemed to trigger something in him. He turned about and said, "Ha! Industrial civilizations, *ja,* maybe so. Not only the pest-begotten Adderkops ply this region of space. Gives some chance perhaps we can come in detection range of an un-beat-up ship, *nie?* You go get Yamamura to jack up our detector sensitivities till we can feel a gnat twiddle its wings back in my Djakarta office on Earth, so lazy the cleaners are. Then we go off this direct course and run a standard naval search pattern at reduced speed."

"And if we find a ship? Could belong to the enemy, you know."

"That chance we take."

"In all events, sir, we'll lose time. The pursuit will gain on us while we follow a search-helix. Especially if we spend days persuading some nonhmuan crew who've never heard of the human race, that we have to be taken to Valhalla immediately if not sooner."

"We burn that bridge when we come to it. You have might be a more hopeful scheme?"

"Well . . ." Torrance pondered a while, blackly.

The steward came in with a fresh tankard. Van Rijn snatched it.

"I think you're right, sir," said Torrance. "I'll go and—"

"Virginal!" bellowed Van Rijn.

Torrance jumped. "What?"

"Virginal! That's the word I was looking for. The first beer of the day, you idiot!"

The cabin door chimed. Torrance groaned. He'd been hoping for some sleep, at least, after more hours on deck than he cared to number. But when the ship prowled through darkness, seeking another ship which might or might not be out there, and the hunters drew closer . . . "Come in."

Jeri Kofoed entered. Torrance gaped, sprang to his feet, and bowed. "Freelady! What—what—what a surprise! Is there anything I can do?"

"Please." She laid a hand on his. Her gown was of shimmerite and shameless in cut, because Van Rijn hadn't provided any other sort, but the look she gave Torrance had nothing to do with that. "I had to come, Lodge-master. If you've any pity at all, you'll listen to me."

He waved her to a chair, offered cigarettes, and struck one for himself. The smoke, drawn deep into his lungs, calmed him a little. He sat down on the opposite side of the table. "If I can be of help to you, Freelady Kofoed, you know I'm happy to oblige. Uh . . . Freeman Van Rijn . . ."

"He's asleep. Not that he has any claims on me. I haven't signed a contract or any such thing." Her irritation gave way to a wry smile. "Oh, admitted, we're all his inferiors, in fact as well as in status. I'm not contravening his wishes, not really. It's just that he won't answer my questions, and if I don't find out what's going on I'll have to start screaming."

Torrance weighed a number of factors. A private explanation, in more detail than the crew had required, might indeed be best for her. "As you wish, Freelady," he said, and related what had happened to the converter. "We can't fix it ourselves," he concluded. "If we continued traveling at high quasi-speed, we'd burn it out before we arrived; and then, without power, we'd soon die. If we proceed slowly enough to preserve it, we'd need half a year to reach Valhalla, which is more time than we have supplies for. Though the Adderkops would doubtless track us down within a week or two."

She shivered. "Why? I don't understand." She stared at her glowing cigarette end for a moment, until a degree of composure returned, and with it a touch of humor. "I may pass for a fast, sophisticated girl on Freya, Captain. But you know even better than I, Freya is a jerkwater planet on the very fringe of human civilization. We've hardly any spatial traffic, except the League merchant ship and they never stay long in port. I really know nothing about military or political technology. No one told me this was anything more important than a scouting mission, because I never thought to inquire. Why should the Adderkops be so anxious to catch us?"

Torrance considered the total picture before framing a reply. As a spaceman of the League, he must make an effort before he could appreciate how little the enemy actually meant to colonists who seldom left their home world. The name "Adderkop" was Freyan, a term of scorn for outlaws who'd been booted off the planet a century ago. Since then, however, the Freyans had had no direct contact with them. Somewhere in the unexplored deeps beyond Valhalla, the fugitives had settled on some unknown planet. Over the generations, their numbers grew, and so did the numbers of their warships. But Freya was still too strong for them to raid, and had no extraplanetary enterprises of her own to be harried. Why should Freya care?

Torrance decided to explain systematically, even if he must repeat the obvious. "Well," he said, "the Adderkops aren't stupid. They keep somewhat in touch with events, and know the Polesotechnic League wants to expand its operations into this region. They don't like that. It'd mean the end of their attacks on planets which can't fight back, their squeezing of tribute and their overpriced trade. Not that the League is composed of saints; we don't tolerate that sort of thing, but merely because freebooting cuts into the profits of our member companies. So the Adderkops undertook, not to fight a full-dress war against us, but to harass our outposts till we gave it up as a bad job. They have the advantage of knowing their own sector of space, which we hardly do at all. And we were, indeed, at the point of writing this whole region off and trying someplace else. Freeman Van Rijn wanted to make one last attempt. The opposition to doing so was so great that he had to come here and lead the expedition himself.

"I suppose you know what he did. Used an unholy skill at bribery and bluff, at extracting what little information the prisoners we'd taken possessed, at fitting odd facts together. He got a clue to a hitherto untried segment. We flitted there, picked up a neutrino trail, and followed it to a human-colonized planet. As you know, it's almost certainly their own home world.

"If we bring back that information, there'll be no more trouble with the Adderkops. Not after the League sends in a few Star class battleships and threatens to bombard their planet. They realize as much. We were spotted; several warcraft jumped us; we were lucky enough to get away. Their ships are obsolete, and so far we've shown them a clean pair of heels. But I hardly think they've quit hunting for us. They'll send their entire fleet cruising in search. Hyperdrive vibrations transmit instantaneously, and can be detected up to about one light-year distance. So if any Adderkop picks up our 'wake' and homes in on it— with us crippled—that's the end."

She drew hard on her cigarette, but remained otherwise calm. "What are your plans?"

"A countermove. Instead of trying to make Freya—uh —I mean, we're proceeding in a search-helix at medium speed, straining our own detectors. If we discover another ship, we'll use the last gasp of our engine to close in. If it's an Adderkop vessel, well, perhaps we can seize it or something; we do have a couple of light guns in our turrets. It may be a nonhuman craft, though. Our intelligence reports, interrogation of prisoners, evaluation of explorers' observations, and so on, all indicate that three or four different species in this region possess the hyperdrive. The Adderkops themselves aren't certain about all of them. Space is so damned *huge*."

"If it does turn out to be nonhuman?"

"Then we'll do what seems indicated."

"I see." Her bright head nodded. She sat for a while, unspeaking, before she dazzled him with a smile. "Thanks, Captain. You don't know how much you've helped me."

Torrance suppressed a foolish grin. "A pleasure, Freelady."

"I'm coming to Earth with you. Did you know that? Freeman Van Rijn has promised me a very good job."

He always does, thought Torrance.

Jeri leaned closer. "I hope we'll have a chance on the Earthward trip to get better acquainted, Captain. Or even right now."

The alarm bell chose that moment to ring.

The *Hebe G.B.* was a yacht, not a buccaneer frigate. When Nicholas van Rijn was aboard, though, the distinction sometimes got a little blurred. So she had more legs than most ships, detectors of uncommon sensitivity, and a crew experienced in the tactics of overhauling.

She was able to get a bearing on the hyperemission of the other craft long before her own vibrations were observed. Pacing the unseen one, she established the set course it was following, then poured on all available juice to intercept. If the stranger had maintained quasivelocity, there would have been contact in three or four hours. Instead, its wake indicated a sheering off, an attempt to flee. The *Hebe G.B.* changed course, too, and continued gaining on her slower quarry.

"They're afraid of us," decided Torrance. "And they're not running back toward the Adderkop sun. Which two facts indicate they're not Adderkops themselves, but do have reason to be scared of strangers." He nodded, rather grimly, for during the preliminary investigations he had inspected a few backward planets which the bandit nation had visited.

Seeing that the pursuer kept shortening her distance, the pursued turned off their hyperdrive. Reverting to intrinsic sublight velocity, converter throttled down to minimal output, their ship became an infinitesimal speck in an effectively infinite space. The maneuver often works; after casting about futilely for a while, the enemy gives up and goes home. The *Hebe G.B.*, though, was prepared. The known superlight vector, together with the instant of cutoff, gave her computers a rough idea of where the prey was. She continued to that volume of space and then hopped about in a well-designed search pattern, reverting to normal state at intervals to sample the neutrino haze which any nuclear engine emits. Those nuclear engines known as stars provided most; but by statistical analysis, the computers presently isolated one feeble nearby source. The yacht went thither . . . and wan against the glittering sky, the other ship appeared in her screens.

It was several times her size, a cylinder with bluntly rounded nose and massive drive cones, numerous housings for auxiliary boats, a single gun turret. The principles of physics dictate that the general conformation of all ships intended for a given purpose shall be roughly the same. But any spaceman could see that this one had never been built by members of Technic civilization.

Fire blazed. Even with the automatic stopping-down of his viewscreen, Torrance was momentarily blinded. Instruments told him that the stranger had fired a fusion shell which his own robogunners had intercepted with a missile. The attack had been miserably slow and feeble. This was not a warcraft in any sense; it was no more a match for the *Hebe G.B.* than the yacht was for one of the Adderkops chasing her.

"Hokay, now we got that foolishness out of the way and we can talk business," said Van Rijn. "Get them on the telecom and develop a common language. Fast! Then explain we mean no harm but want just a lift to Valhalla." He hesitated before adding, with a distinct wince, "We can pay well."

"Might prove difficult, sir," said Torrance. "Our ship is identifiably human-built, but chances are that the only humans they've ever met are Adderkops."

"Well, so if it makes needful, we can board them and force them to transport us, *nie?* Hurry up, for Satan's sake! If we wait too long here, like bebobbled snoozers, we'll get caught."

Torrance was about to point out they were safe enough. The Adderkops were far behind the swifter Terrestrial ship. They could have no idea that her hyperdrive was now cut off; when they began to suspect it, they could have no measurable probability of finding her. Then he

remembered that the case was not so simple. If the par-
leying with these strangers took unduly long—more than a
week, at best—Adderkop squadrons would have pene-
trated this general region and gone beyond. They would
probably remain on picket for months: which the humans
could not do for lack of food. When a hyperdrive did start
up, they'd detect it and run down this awkward merchant-
man with ease. The only hope was to hitch a ride to Valhalla *soon,* using the head start already gained to offset the
disadvantage of reduced speed.

"We're trying all bands, sir," he said. "No response so
far." He frowned worriedly. "I don't understand. They
must know we've got them cold, and they must have
picked up our calls and realize we want to talk. Why don't
they respond? Wouldn't cost them anything."

"Maybe they abandoned ship," suggested the communications officer. "They might have hyperdriven lifeboats."

"No." Torrance shook his head. "We'd have spotted
that. . . . Keep trying, Freeman Betancourt. If we haven't
gotten an answer in an hour, we'll lay alongside and
board."

The receiver screens remained blank. But at the end of
the grace period, when Torrance was issuing space armor,
Yamamura reported something new. Neutrino output
had increased from a source near the stern of the alien.
Some process involving moderate amounts of energy was
being carried out.

Torrance clamped down his helmet. "We'll have a look
at that."

He posted a skeleton crew—Van Rijn himself, loudly
protesting, took over the bridge—and led his boarding
party to the main air lock. Smooth as a gliding shark (the
old swine was a blue-ribbon spaceman after all, the captain realized in some astonishment), the *Hebe G.B.*
clamped on a tractor beam and hauled herself toward the
bigger vessel.

It disappeared. Recoil sent the yacht staggering.

"Beelzebub and botulism!" snarled Van Rijn. "He went

back into hyper, ha? We see about that!" The ulcerated
converter shrieked as he called upon it, but the engines
were given power. On a lung and a half, the Terrestrial
ship again overtook the foreigner. Van Rijn phased in so
casually that Torrance almost forgot this was a job considered difficult by master pilots. He evaded a frantic pres-
sor beam and tied his yacht to the larger hull with un-
shearable bands of force. He cut off his hyperdrive again,
for the converter couldn't take much more. Being within
the force-field of the alien, the *Hebe G.B.* was carried
along, though the "drag" of extra mass reduced quasi-
speed considerably. If he had hoped the grappled vessel
would quit and revert to normal state, he was disappoin-
ted. The linked hulls continued plunging faster than light,
toward an unnamed constellation.

Torrance bit back an oath, summoned his men, and
went outside.

He had never forced entry on a hostile craft before, but
assumed it wasn't much different from burning his way
into a derelict. Having chosen his spot, he set up a balloon
tent to conserve air; no use killing the alien crew. The
torches of his men spewed flame; blue actinic sparks
fountained backward and danced through zero gravity.
Meanwhile the rest of the squad stood by with blasters
and grenades.

Beyond, the curves of the two hulls dropped off to infin-
ity. Without compensating electronic viewscreens, the sky
was weirdly distorted by aberration and Doppler effect, as
if the men were already dead and beating through the
other existence toward Judgment. Torrance held his mind
firmly to practical worries. Once inboard, the nonhumans
made prisoner, how was he to communicate? Especially
if he first had to gun down several of them . . .

The outer shell was peeled back. He studied the inner
structure of the plate with fascination. He'd never seen
anything like it before. Surely this race had developed
space travel quite independently of mankind. Though
their engineering must obey the same natural laws, it

was radically different in detail. What was that tough but corky substance lining the inner shell? And was the circuitry embedded in it, for he didn't see any elsewhere?

The last defense gave way. Torrance swallowed hard and shot a flashbeam into the interior. Darkness and vacuum met him. When he entered the hull, he floated, weightless; artificial gravity had been turned off. The crew was hiding someplace and . . .

And . . .

Torrance returned to the yacht in an hour. When he came on the bridge, he found Van Rijn seated by Jeri. The girl started to speak, took a closer look at the captain's face, and clamped her teeth together.

"Well?" snapped the merchant peevishly.

Torrance cleared his throat. His voice sounded unfamiliar and faraway to him. "I think you'd better come have a look, sir."

"You found the crew, wherever the sputtering hell they holed up? What are they like? What kind of ship is this we've gotten us, ha?"

Torrance chose to answer the last question first. "It seems to be an interstellar animal collector's transport vessel. The main hold is full of cages—environmentally controlled compartments, I should say—with the damnedest assortment of creatures I've ever seen outside Luna City Zoo."

"So what the pox is that to me? Where is the collector himself, and his fig-plucking friends?"

"Well, sir." Torrance gulped. "We're pretty sure by now, they're hiding from us. Among all the other animals."

A tube was run between the yacht's main lock and the entry cut into the other ship. Through this, air was pumped and electric lines were strung, to illuminate the prize. By some fancy juggling with the gravitic generator of the *Hebe G.B.*, Yamamura supplied about one-fourth Earth-weight to the foreigner, though he couldn't get the direction uniform and its decks felt canted in wildly varying degrees.

Even under such conditions, Van Rijn walked ponderously. He stood with a salami in one hand and a raw onion in the other, glaring around the captured bridge. It could only be that, though it was in the bows rather then the waist. The viewscreens were still in operation: smaller than human eyes found comfortable, but revealing the same pattern of stars, surely by the same kind of optical compensators. A control console made a semicircle at the forward bulkhead, too big for a solitary human to operate. Yet presumably the designer had only had one pilot in mind, for a single seat had been placed in the middle of the arc.

Had been. A short metal post rose from the deck. Similar structures stood at other points, and boltholes showed where chairs were once fastened to them. But the seats had been removed.

"Pilot sat there at the center, I'd guess, when they weren't simply running on automatic," Torrance hazarded. "Navigator and communications officer . . . here and here? I'm not sure. Anyhow, they probably didn't use a copilot, but that chair bollard at the after end of the room suggests that an extra officer sat in reserve, ready to take over."

Van Rijn munched his onion and tugged his goatee. "Pestish big, this panel," he said. "Must be a race of bloody-bedamned octopussies, ha? Look how complicated."

He waved the salami around the half circle. The console, which seemed to be of some fluorocarbon polymer, held very few switches or buttons, but scores of flat luminous plates, each about twenty centimeters square. Some of them were depressed. Evidently these were the controls. Cautious experiment had shown that a stiff push was needed to budge them. The experiment had ended then and there, for the ship's cargo lock had opened and a good deal of air was lost before Torrance slapped the plate he had been testing hard enough to make the hull reseal itself. One should not tinker with the atomic-powered unknown; most especially not in galactic space.

"They must be strong like horses, to steer by this

system without getting exhausted," went on Van Rijn. "The size of everything tells likewise, *nie?*"

"Well, not exactly, sir," said Torrance. "The viewscreens seem made for dwarfs. The meters even more so." He pointed to a bank of instruments, no larger than buttons, on each of which a single number glowed. (Or letter, or ideogram, or what? They looked vaguely Old Chinese.) Occasionally a symbol changed value. "A human couldn't use these long without severe eyestrain. Of course, having eyes better adapted to close work than ours doesn't prove they are not giants. Certainly that switch couldn't be reached from here without long arms, and it seems meant for big hands." By standing on tiptoe, he touched it himself: an outsize double-pole affair set overhead, just above the pilot's hypothetical seat.

The switch fell open.

A roar came from aft. Torrance lurched backward under a sudden force. He caught at a shelf on the after bulkhead to steady himself. Its thin metal buckled as he clutched. "Devilfish and dunderheads!" cried Van Rijn. Bracing his columnar legs, he reached up and shoved the switch back into position. The noise ended. Normality returned. Torrance hastened to the bridge doorway, a tall arch, and shouted down the corridor beyond: "It's okay! Don't worry! We've got it under control!"

"What the blue blinking blazes happened?" demanded Van Rijn, in somewhat more high-powered words.

Torrance mastered a slight case of the shakes. "Emergency switch, I'd say." His tone wavered. "Turns on the gravitic field full speed ahead, not wasting any force on acceleration compensators. Of course, we being in hyperdrive, it wasn't very effective. Only gave us a—uh—less than one G push, intrinsic. In normal state we'd have accelerated several Gs, at least. It's for quick getaways and . . . and . . ."

"And you, with brains like fermented gravy and bananas for fingers, went ahead and yanked it open!"

Torrance felt himself redden. "How was I to know, sir?

I must've applied less than half a kilo of force. Emergency switches aren't hair-triggered, after all! Considering how much it takes to move one of those control plates, who'd have thought the switch would respond to so little?"

Van Rijn took a closer look. "I see now there is a hook to secure it by," he said. "Must be they use that when the ship's on a high-gravity planet." He peered down a hole near the center of the panel, about one centimeter in diameter and fifteen deep. At the bottom a small key projected. "This must be another special control, ha? Safer than that switch. You would need thin-nosed pliers to make a turning of it." He scratched his pomaded curls. "But then why is not the pliers hanging handy? I don't see even a hook or bracket or drawer for them."

"I don't care," said Torrance. "When the whole interior's been stripped— There's nothing but a slagheap in the engine room, I tell you, fused metal, carbonized plastic . . . bedding, furniture, anything they thought might give us a clue to their identity, all melted down in a jury-rigged cauldron. They used their own converter to supply heat. That was the cause of the neutrino flux Yamamura observed. They must have worked like demons."

"But they did not destroy all needful tools and machines, surely? Simpler then they should blow up their whole ship, and us with it. I was sweating like a hog, me, for fear they would do that. Not so good a way for a poor sinful old man to end his days, blown into radioactive stinks three hundred light-years from the vineyards of Earth."

"N-n-no. As far as we can tell from a cursory examination, they didn't sabotage anything absolutely vital. We can't be sure, of course. Yamamura's gang would need weeks just to get a general idea of how this ship is put together, let alone the practical details of operating it. But I agree, the crew isn't bent on suicide. They've got us more neatly trapped than they know, even. Bound helplessly through space—toward their home star, maybe—in any event, almost at right angles to the course we want."

Torrance led the way out. "Suppose we go have a more thorough look at the zoo, sir," he went on. "Yamamura talked about setting up some equipment . . . to help us tell the crew from the animals!"

The main hold comprised almost half the volume of the great ship. A corridor below, a catwalk above, ran through a double row of two-decker cubicles. These numbered ninety-six, and were identical. Each was about five meters on a side, with adjustable fluorescent plates in the ceiling and a springy, presumably inert plastic on the floor. Shelves and parallel bars ran along the side walls, for the benefit of animals that liked jumping or climbing. The rear wall was connected to well-shielded machines; Yamamura didn't dare tamper with these, but said they obviously regulated atmosphere, temperature, gravity, sanitation, and other environmental factors within each "cage." The front wall, facing on corridor and catwalk, was transparent. It held a stout air lock, almost as high as the cubicle itself, motorized but controlled by simple wheels inside and out. Only a few compartments were empty.

The humans had not strung fluoros in this hold, for it wasn't necessary. Torrance and Van Rijn walked through shadows, among monsters; the simulated light of a dozen different suns streamed around them: red, orange, yellow, greenish, and harsh electric blue.

A thing like a giant shark, save that tendrils fluttered about its head, swam in a water-filled cubicle among fronded seaweeds. Next to it was a cageful of tiny flying reptiles, their scales aglitter in prismatic hues, weaving and dodging through the air. On the opposite side, four mammals crouched among yellow mists: beautiful creatures, the size of a bear, vividly tiger-striped, walking mostly on all fours but occasionally standing up; then you noticed the retractable claws between stubby fingers, and the carnivore jaws on the massive heads. Farther on the humans passed half a dozen sleek red beasts like six-legged otters, frolicking in a tank of water provided for them. The environmental machines must have decided this was their feeding time, for a hopper spewed chunks of proteinaceous material into a trough and the animals lolloped over to rip it with their fangs.

"Automatic feeding," Torrance observed. "I think probably the food is synthesized on the spot, according to the specifications of each individual species as determined by biochemical methods. For the crew, also. At least, we haven't found anything like a galley."

Van Rijn shuddered. "Nothing but synthetics? Not even a little glass Genever before dinner?" He brightened. "Ha, maybe here we find a good new market. And until they learn the situation, we can charge them triple prices."

"First," clipped Torrance, "we've got to find them."

Yamamura stood near the middle of the hold, focusing a set of instruments on a certain cage. Jeri stood by, handing him what he asked for, plugging and unplugging at a small powerpack. Van Rijn hove into view. "What goes on, anyhows?" he asked.

The chief engineer turned a patient brown face to him. "I've got the rest of the crew examining the ship in detail, sir," he said. "I'll join them as soon as I've gotten Freelady Kofoed trained at this particular job. She can handle the routine of it while the rest of us use our special skills to . . ." His words trailed off. He grinned ruefully. "To poke and prod gizmos we can't possibly understand in less than a month of work, with our limited research tools."

"A month we have not got," said Van Rijn. "You are here checking conditions inside each individual cage?"

"Yes, sir. They're metered, of course, but we can't read the meters, so we have to do the job ourselves. I've haywired this stuff together, to give an approximate value of gravity, atmospheric pressure and composition, temperature, illumination spectrum, and so forth. It's slow work, mostly because of all the arithmetic needed to turn the dial readings into such data. Luckily, we don't have to test every cubicle, or even most of them."

"No," said Van Rijn. "Even to a union organizer, obvious this ship was never made by fishes or birds. In fact, some kind of hands is always necessary."

"Or tentacles." Yamamura nodded at the compartment before him. The light within was dim red. Several black creatures could be seen walking restlessly about. They had stumpy-legged quadrupedal bodies, from which torsos rose, centaur-fashion, toward heads armored in some bony material. Below the faceless heads were six thick, ropy arms, set in triplets. Two of these ended in three boneless but probably strong finger.

"I suspect these are our coy friends," said Yamamura. "If so, we'll have a deuce of a time. They breathe hydrogen under high pressure and triple gravity, at a temperature of seventy below."

"Are they the only ones who like that kind of weather?" asked Torrance.

Yamamura gave him a sharp look. "I see what you're getting at, skipper. No, they aren't. In the course of putting this apparatus together and testing it, I've already found three other cubicles where conditions are similar. And in those, the animals are obviously just animals: snakes and so on, which couldn't possibly have built this ship."

"But then these octopus-horses can't be the crew, can they?" asked Jeri timidly. "I mean, if the crew were collecting animals from other planets, they wouldn't take home animals along, would they?"

"They might," said Van Rijn. "We have a cat and a couple parrots aboard the *Hebe G.B., nie?* Or, there are many planets with very similar conditions of the hydrogen sort, just like Earth and Freya are much-alike oxygen planets. So that proves nothings." He turned toward Yamamura, rather like a rotating globe himself. "But see here, even if the crew did pump out all the air before we boarded, why not check their reserve tanks? If we find air stored away just like these diddlers here are breathing . . ."

"I thought of that," said Yamamura. "In fact, it was

almost the first thing I told the men to look for. They've located nothing. I don't think they'll have any success, either. Because what they did find was an adjustable catalytic manifold. At least, it looks as if it should be, though we'd need days to find out for certain. Anyhow, my guess is that it renews exhausted air and acts as a chemosynthesizer to replace losses from a charge of simple inorganic compounds. The crew probably bled all the ship's air into space before we boarded. When we go away, if we do, they'll open the door of their particular cage a crack, so its air can trickle out. The environmental adjuster will automatically force the chemosynthesizer to replace this. Eventually the ship'll be full of enough of their kind of air for them to venture forth and adjust things more precisely." He shrugged. "That's assuming they even need to. Perhaps Earth-type conditions suit them perfectly well."

"Uh, yes," said Torrance. "Suppose we look around some more, and line up the possibly intelligent species."

Van Rijn trundled along with him. "What sort intelligence they got, these bespattered aliens?" he grumbled. "Why try this stupid masquerade in the first places?"

"It's not too stupid to have worked so far," said Torrance dryly. "We're being carried along on a ship we don't know how to stop. They must hope we'll either give up and depart, or else that we'll remain baffled until the ship enters their home region. At which time, quite probably a naval vessel—or whatever they've got—will detect us, close in, and board us to check up on what's happened."

He paused before a compartment. "I wonder . . ."

The quadruped within was the size of an elephant, though with a more slender build indicating a lower gravity than Earth's. Its skin was green and faintly scaled, a ruff of hair along the back. The eyes with which it looked out were alert and enigmatic. It had an elephant-like trunk, terminating in a ring of pseudodactyls which must be as strong and sensitive as human fingers.

"How much could a one-armed race accomplish?"

mused Torrance. "About as much as we, I imagine, if not quite as easily. And sheer strength would compensate. That trunk could bend an iron bar."

Van Rijn grunted and went past a cubicle of feathered ungulates. He stopped before the next one. "Now here are some beasts might do," he said. "We had one like them on Earth once. What they called it? Quintilla? No, gorilla. Or chimpanzee, better, of gorilla size."

Torrance felt his heart thud. Two adjoining sections each held four animals of a kind which looked extremely hopeful. They were bipedal, short-legged and long-armed. Standing two meters tall, with a three-meter arm span, one of them could certainly operate that control console alone. The wrists, thick as a man's thighs, ended in proportionate hands, four-digited including a true thumb. The three-toed feet were specialized for walking, like man's feet. Their bodies were covered with brown fleece. Their heads were comparatively small, rising almost to a point, with massive snouts and beady eyes under cavernous brow ridges. As they wandered aimlessly about, Torrance saw that they were divided among males and females. On the sides of each neck he noticed two lumens closed by sphincters. The light upon them was the familiar yellowish-white of a Sol-type star.

He forced himself to say, "I'm not sure. Those huge jaws must demand corresponding maxillary muscles, attaching to a ridge on top of the skull. Which'd restrict the cranial capacity."

"Suppose they got brains in their bellies," said Van Rijn.

"Well, some people do," murmured Torrance. As the merchant choked, he added in haste, "No, actually, sir, that's hardly believable. Neural paths would get too long, and so forth. Every animal I know of, if it has a central nervous system at all, keeps the brain close to the principal sense organs: which are usually located in the head. To be sure, a relatively small brain, within limits, doesn't mean these creatures are not intelligent. Their neurones might well be more efficient than ours."

"Humph and hassenpfeffer!" said Van Rijn. "Might, might, might!" As they continued among strange shapes: "We can't go too much by atmosphere or light, either. If hiding, the crew could vary conditions quite a bit from their norm without hurting themselves. Gravity, too, by twenty or thirty percent."

"I hope they breathe oxygen, though—Hoy!" Torrance stopped. After a moment, he realized what was so eerie about the several forms under the orange glow. They were chitinous-armored, not much bigger than a squarish military helmet and about the same shape. Four stumpy legs projected from beneath to carry them awkwardly about on taloned feet; also a pair of short tentacles ending in a bush of cilia. There was nothing special about them, as extra-Terrestrial animals go, except the two eyes which gazed from beneath each helmet: as large and somehow human as—well—the eyes of an octopus.

"Turtles," snorted Van Rijn. "Armadillos at most."

"There can't be any harm in letting Jer—Miss Kofoed check their environment too," said Torrance.

"It can waste time."

"I wonder what they eat. I don't see any mouths."

"Those tentacles look like capillary suckers. I bet they are parasites, or overgrown leeches, or something else like one of my competitors. Come along."

"What do we do after we've established which species could possibly be the crew?" asked Torrance. "Try to communicate with each in turn?"

"Not much use, that. They hide because they don't want to communicate. Unless we can prove to them we are not Adderkops. . . . But hard to see how."

"Wait! Why'd they conceal themselves at all, if they've had contact with the Adderkops? It wouldn't work."

"I think I tell you that, by damn," said Van Rijn. "To give them a name, let us call this unknown race the Eksers. So. The Eksers been traveling space for some time, but space is so big they never bumped into humans. Then the Adderkop nation arises, in this sector where humans never was before. The Eksers hear about this awful new species which has gotten into space also. They land on primitive planets where Adderkops have made raids, talk to natives, maybe plant automatic cameras where they think raids will soon come, maybe spy on Adderkop camps from afar or capture a lone Adderkop ship. So they know what humans look like, but not much else. They do not want humans to know about them, so they shun contact; they are not looking for trouble. Not before they are all prepared to fight a war, at least. Hell's sputtering griddles! Torrance, we have *got* to establish our bona fides with this crew, so they take us to Freya and afterward go tell their leaders all humans are not so bad as the slime-begotten Adderkops. Otherwise, maybe we wake up one day with some planets attacked by Eksers, and before the fighting ends, we have spent billions of credits!" He shook his fists in the air and bellowed like a wounded bull. "It is our duty to prevent this!"

"Our first duty is to get home alive, I'd say," Torrance answered curtly. "I have a wife and kids."

"Then stop throwing sheepish eyes at Jeri Kofoed. I saw her first."

The search turned up one more possibility. Four organisms the length of a man and the build of thick-legged caterpillars dwelt under greenish light. Their bodies were dark blue, spotted with silver. A torso akin to that of the tentacled centauroids, but stockier, carried two true arms. The hands lacked thumbs, but six fingers arranged around a three-quarter circle could accomplish much the same things. Not that adequate hands prove effective intelligence; on Earth, not only simians but a number of reptiles and amphibia boast as much, even if man has the best, and man's apish ancestors were as well-equipped in this respect as we are today. However, the round flat-faced heads of these beings, the large bright eyes beneath feathery antennae of obscure function, the small jaws and delicate lips, all looked promising.

Promising of what? thought Torrance.

Three Earth-days later, he hurried down a central corridor toward the Ekser engine room.

The passage was a great hemicylinder lined with the same rubbery gray plastic as the cages, so that footfalls were silent and spoken words weirdly unresonant. But a deeper vibration went through it, the almost subliminal drone of the hyperengine, driving the ship into darkness toward an unknown star, and announcing their presence to any hunter straying within a light-year of them. The fluoros strung by the humans were far apart, so that one passed through bands of humming shadow. Doorless rooms opened off the hallway. Some were still full of supplies, and however peculiar the shape of tools and containers might be, however unguessable their purpose, this was a reassurance that one still lived, was not yet a ghost aboard the Flying Dutchman. Other cabins, however, had been inhabited. And their bareness made Torrance's skin crawl.

Nowhere did a personal trace remain. Books, both folio and micro, survived, but in the finely printed symbology of a foreign planet. Empty places on the shelves suggested that all illustrated volumes had been sacrificed. Certainly one could see where pictures stuck on the walls had been ripped down. In the big private cabins, in the still larger one which might have been a saloon, as well as in the engine room and workshop and bridge, only the bollards to which furniture had been bolted were left. Long low niches and small cubbyholes were built into the cabin bulkheads, but when all bedding had been thrown into a white-hot cauldron, how could one guess which were the bunks . . . if either kind were? Clothing, ornaments, cooking and eating utensils, everything was destroyed. One room must have been a lavatory, but all the facilities had been ripped out. Another might have been used for scientific studies, presumably of captured animals, but was so gutted that no human was certain.

By God, you've got to admire them, Torrance thought. Captured by beings whom they had every reason to think of as conscienceless monsters, the aliens had not taken the easy way out, the atomic explosion that would annihilate both crews. They might have, except for the chance of this being a zoo ship. But given a hope of survival, they snatched it, with an imaginative daring few humans could have matched. Now they sat in plain view, waiting for the monsters to depart—without wrecking their ship in mere spitefulness—or for a naval vessel of their own to rescue them. They had no means of knowing their captors were not Adderkops, or that this sector would soon be filled with Adderkop squadrons; the bandits rarely ventured even this close to Valhalla. Within the limits of available information, the aliens were acting with complete logic. But the nerve it took!

I wish we could identify them and make friends, thought Torrance. The Eksers would be damned good friends for Earth to have. Or Ramanujan, or Freya, or the entire Polesotechnic League.—With a lopsided grin: I'll bet they'd be nowhere near as easy to swindle as Old Nick thinks. They might well swindle him. That I'd love to see!

My reason is more personal, though, he thought with a return of bleakness. If we don't clear up this misunderstanding soon, neither they nor we will be around. I mean *soon*. If we have another three or four days of grace, we're lucky.

The passage opened on a well, with ramps curving down either side to a pair of automatic doors. One door led to the engine room, Torrance knew. Behind it, a nuclear converter powered the ship's electrical system, gravitic cones, and hyperdrive; the principles on which this was done were familiar to him, but the actual machines were enigmas cased in metal and in foreign symbols. He took the other door, which opened on a workshop. A good deal of the equipment here was identifiable, however distorted to his eyes: lathe, drill press, oscilloscope, crystal tester. Much else was mystery. Yamamura sat at an improvised workbench, fitting together a piece of electronic apparatus. Several other devices, haywired on breadboards,

stood close by. His face was shockingly haggard, and his
hands trembled. He'd been working this whole time, with
stimpills to keep him awake.

As Torrance approached, the engineer was talking with
Betancourt, the communications man. The entire crew
of the *Hebe G.B.* were under Yamamura's direction, in a
frantic attempt to outflank the Eksers by learning on their
own how to operate this ship.

"I've identified the basic electrical arrangement, sir,"
Betancourt was saying. "They don't tap the converter
directly, like us; so evidently they haven't developed
our stepdown methods. Instead, they use a heat ex-
changer to run an extremely large generator—yeah, the
same thing you guessed was an armature-type dynamo—
and draw A.C. for the ship off that. Where D.C. is needed,
the A.C. passes through a set of rectifier plates which, by
looking at 'em, I'm sure must be copper oxide. They're
bare, behind a safety screen, though so much current goes
through that they're too hot to look at close up. It all
seems kind of primitive to me."

"Or else merely different," sighed Yamamura. "We use
a light-element-fusion converter, one of whose advantages
is that it can develop electric current directly. They may
have perfected a power plant which utilizes moderately
heavy elements with small positive packing fractions.
I remember that was tried on Earth a long while ago, and
given up as impractical. But maybe the Eksers are better
engineers than us. Such a system would have the advantage of needing less refinement of fuel—which'd be a
real advantage to a ship knocking about among unexplored
planets. Maybe enough to justify that clumsy heat ex-
changer and rectifier system. We simply don't know."

He stared head-shakingly at the wires he was soldering.
"We don't know a damn thing," he said. Seeing Torrance:
"Well, carry on, Freeman Betancourt. And remember,
festina lente."

"For fear of wrecking the ship?" asked the captain.

Yamamura nodded. "The Eksers would've known a

small craft like ours couldn't generate a big enough hyper-force field to tug their own ship home," he replied. "So they'll have made sure no prize crew could make off with it. Some of the stuff may be booby-trapped to wreck itself if it isn't handled just so; and how'd we ever make repairs? Hence we're proceeding with the utmost caution. So cautiously that we haven't a prayer of figuring out the controls before the Adderkops find us."

"It keeps the crew busy, though."

"Which is useful. Uh-huh. Well, sir, I've about got my basic apparatus set up. Everything seems to test okay. Now let me know which animal you want to investigate first." As Torrance hesitated, the engineer explained: "I have to adapt the equipment for the creature in question, you see. Especially if it's a hydrogen breather."

Torrance shook his head. "Oxygen. In fact, they live under conditions so much like ours that we can walk right into their cages. The gorilloids. That's what Jeri and I have named them. Those woolly, two-meter-tall bipeds with the ape faces."

Yamamura made an ape face of his own. "Brutes that powerful? Have they shown any sign of intelligence?"

"No. But then, would you expect the Eksers to do so? Jeri Kofoed and I have been parading in front of the cages of all the possible species, making signs, drawing pictures, everything we could think of, trying to get the message across that we are not Adderkops and the genuine article is chasing us. No luck, of course. All the animals did give us an interested regard except the gorilloids . . . which may or may not prove anything."

"What animals, now? I've been so blinking busy—"

"Well, we call 'em the tiger apes, the tentacle centaurs, the elephantoid, the helmet beasts, and the caterpiggles. That's stretching things, I know; the tiger apes and the helmet beasts are highly improbable, to say the least, and the elephantoid isn't much more convincing. The gorilloids have the right size and the most efficient-looking hands, and they're oxygen breathers as I said, so we may as well take them first. Next in order of likelihood, I'd guess, are the caterpiggles and the tentacle centaurs. But the caterpiggles, though oxygen breathers, are from a high-gravity planet; their air pressure would give us narcosis in no time. The tentacle centaurs breathe hydrogen. In either case, we'd have to work in space armor."

"The gorilloids will be quite bad enough, thank you kindly!"

Torrance looked at the workbench. "What exactly do you plan to do?" he asked. "I've been too busy with my own end of this affair to learn any details of yours."

"I've adapted some things from the medical kit," said Yamamura. "A sort of ophthalmoscope, for example; because the ship's instruments use color codes and finely printed symbols, so that the Eksers are bound to have eyes at least as good as ours. Then this here's a nervous-impulse tracer. It detects synaptic flows and casts a three-dimensional image into yonder crystal box, so we can see the whole nervous system functioning as a set of luminous traces. By correlating this with gross anatomy, we can roughly identify the sympathetic and parasympathetic systems—or their equivalents—I hope. And the brain. And, what's really to the point, the degree of brain activity more or less independent of the other nerve paths. That is, whether the animal is thinking."

He shrugged. "It tests out fine on me. Whether it'll work on a nonhuman, especially in a different sort of atmosphere, I do not know. I'm sure it'll develop bugs."

" 'We can but try,' " quoted Torrance wearily.

"I suppose Old Nick is sitting and thinking," said Yamamura in an edged voice. "I haven't seen him for quite some time."

"He's not been helping Jeri and me either," said Torrance. "Told us our attempt to communicate was futile until we could prove to the Eksers that we knew who they were. And even after that, he said, the only communication at first will be by gestures made with a pistol."

"He's probably right."

"He's not right! Logically, perhaps, but not psychologically. Or morally. He sits in his suite with a case of brandy and a box of cigars. The cook, who could be down here helping you, is kept aboard the yacht to fix him his damned gourmet meals. You'd think he didn't care if we're blown out of the sky!"

He remembered his oath of fealty, his official position, and so on and so on. They seemed nonsensical enough, here on the edge of extinction. But habit was strong. He swallowed and said harshly, "Sorry. Please ignore what I said. When you're ready, Freeman Yamamura, we'll test the gorilloids."

Six men and Jeri stood by in the passage with drawn blasters. Torrance hoped fervently they wouldn't have to shoot. He hoped even more that, if they did have to, he'd still be alive.

He gestured to the four crewmen at his back. "Okay, boys." He wet his lips. His heart thuttered. Being a captain and a Lodgemaster was very fine until moments like this came, when you must make a return for all your special privileges.

He spun the outside control wheel. The air-lock motor hummed and opened the doors. He stepped through, into a cage of gorilloids.

Pressure differentials weren't enough to worry about, but after all this time at one-fourth G, to enter a field only ten percent less than Earth's was like a blow. He lurched, almost fell, gasped in an air warm and thick and full of unnamed stenches. Sagging back against the wall, he stared across the floor at the four bipeds. Their brown fleecy bodies loomed unfairly tall, up and up to the coarse faces. Eyes overshadowed by brows glared at him. He clapped a hand on his stun pistol. He didn't want to shoot it, either. No telling what supersonics might do to a nonhuman nervous system; and if these were in truth the crewfolk, the worst thing he could do was inflict serious injury on one of them. But he wasn't used to being small and frail. The knurled handgrip was a comfort.

A male growled, deep in his chest, and advanced a step. His pointed head thrust forward, the sphincters in his neck opened and shut like sucking mouths; his jaws gaped to show the white teeth.

Torrance backed toward a corner. "I'll try to attract that one in the lead away from the others," he called softly. "Then get him."

"Aye." A spacehand, a stocky slant-eyed nomad from Altai, uncoiled a lariat. Behind him, the other three spread a net woven for this purpose.

The gorilloid paused. A female hooted. The male seemed to draw resolution from her. He waved the others back with a strangely human-like gesture and stalked toward Torrance.

The captain drew his stunner, pointed it shakily, resheathed it, and held out both hands. "Friend," he croaked.

His hope that the masquerade might be dropped became suddenly ridiculous. He sprang back toward the air lock. The gorilloid snarled and snatched at him. Torrance wasn't fast enough. The hand ripped his shirt open and left a bloody trail on his breast. He went to hands and knees, stabbed with pain. The Altaian's lasso whirled and snaked forth. Caught around the ankles, the gorilloid crashed. His weight shook the cubicle.

"Get him! Watch out for his arms! Here—"

Torrance staggered back to his feet. Beyond the melee, where four men strove to wind a roaring, struggling monster in a net, he saw the other three creatures. They were crowded into the opposite corner, howling in basso. The compartment was like the inside of a drum.

"Get him out," choked Torrance. "Before the others charge."

He aimed his stunner again. If intelligent, they'd know this was a weapon. They might attack anyway. . . . Deftly, the man from Altai roped an arm, snubbed his lariat around the gargantuan torso, and made it fast by a slip knot. The net came into position. Helpless in cords of wire-strong fiber, the gorilloid was dragged to the entrance. Another male advanced, step by jerky step. Torrance stood his ground. The animal ululation and human shouting surfed about him, within him. His wound throbbed. He saw with unnatural clarity: the muzzle full of teeth that could snap his head off, the little dull eyes turned red with fury, the hands so much like his own but black-skinned, four-fingered, and enormous. . . .

"All clear, skipper!"

The gorilloid lunged. Torrance scrambled through the airlock chamber. The giant followed. Torrance braced himself in the corridor and aimed his stun pistol. The gorilloid halted, shivered, looked around in something resembling bewilderment, and retreated. Torrance closed the air lock.

Then he sat down and trembled.

Jeri bent over him. "Are you all right?" she breathed. "Oh! You've been hurt!"

"Nothing much," he mumbled. "Gimme a cigarette."

She took one from her belt pouch and said with a crispness he admired, "I suppose it is just a bruise and a deep scratch. But we'd better check it, anyway, and sterilize. Might be infected."

He nodded but remained where he was until he had finished the cigarette. Further down the corridor, Yamamura's men got their captive secured to a steel framework. Unharmed but helpless, the brute yelped and tried to bite as the engineer approached with his equipment. Returning him to the cubicle afterward was likely to be almost as tough as getting him out.

Torrance rose. Through the transparent wall, he saw a female gorilloid viciously pulling something to shreds, and realized he had lost his turban when he was knocked over. He sighed. "Nothing much we can do till Yamamura gives us a verdict," he said. "Come on, let's go rest a while."

"Sick bay first," said Jeri firmly. She took his arm. They went to the entry hole, through the tube, and into the steady half-weight of the *Hebe G.B.* which Van Rijn preferred. Little was said while Jeri got Torrance's shirt off, swabbed the wound with universal disinfectant, which stung like hell, and bandaged it. Afterward he suggested a drink.

They entered the saloon. To their surprise, and to Torrance's displeasure, Van Rijn was there. He sat at the inlaid mahogany table, dressed in snuff-stained lace and his usual sarong, a bottle in one hand and a Trichinopoly cigar in the other. A litter of papers lay before him.

"Ah, so," he said, glancing up. "What gives?"

"They're testing a gorilloid now." Torrance flung himself into a chair. Since the steward had been drafted for the capture party, Jeri went after drinks. Her voice floated back, defiant:

"Captain Torrance was almost killed in the process. Couldn't you at least come watch, Nick?"

"What use I should watch, like some tourist with haddock eyes?" scoffed the merchant. "I make no skeletons about it, I am too old and fat to help chase large economy-size apes. Nor am I so technical I can twiddle knobs for Yamamura." He took a puff of his cigar and added complacently, "Besides, that is not my job. I am no kind of specialist, I have no fine university degrees, I learned in the school of hard knockers. But what I learned is how to make men do things for me, and then how to make something profitable from all their doings."

Torrance breathed out, long and slow. With the tension eased, he was beginning to feel immensely tired. "What're you checking over?" he asked.

"Reports of engineer studies on the Ekser ship," said Van Rijn. "I told everybody should take full notes on what they observed. Somewhere in those notes is maybe a clue we can use. If the gorilloids are not the Eksers, I mean. The gorilloids are possible, and I see no way to eliminate them except by Yamamura's checkers."

Torrance rubbed his eyes. "They're not entirely plaus-

ible," he said. "Most of the stuff we've found seems meant
for big hands. But some of the tools, especially, are so
small that—Oh, well, I suppose a nonhuman might be as
puzzled by an assortment of our own tools. Does it really
make sense that the same race would use sledge hammers
and etching needles?"

Jeri came back with two stiff Scotch-and-sodas. His gaze
followed her. In a tight blouse and half knee-length skirt,
she was worth following. She sat down next to him rather
than to Van Rijn, whose jet eyes narrowed.

However, the older man spoke mildly. "I would like if
you should list for me, here and now, the other possibilities, with your reasons for thinking of them. I have seen
them too, natural, but my own ideas are not all clear yet
and maybe something that occurs to you would joggle
my head."

Torrance nodded. One might as well talk shop, even
though he'd been over this ground a dozen times before
with Jeri and Yamamura.

"Well," he said, "the tentacle centaurs appear very
likely. You know the ones I mean. They live under red
light and about half again Earth's gravity. A dim sun and
a low temperature must make it possible for their planet
to retain hydrogen, because that's what they breathe,
hydrogen and argon. You know how they look: bodies
sort of like rhinoceri, torsos with bone-plated heads and
fingered tentacles. Like the gorilloids, they're big enough
to pilot this ship easily.

"All the others are oxygen breathers. The ones we call
caterpiggles—the long, many-legged, blue-and-silver ones,
with the peculiar hands and the particularly intelligent-
looking faces—they're from an oddball world. It must be
big. They're under three Gs in their cage, which can't be a
red herring for this length of time. Body fluid adjustment
would go out of kilter, if they're used to much lower weight.
Even so, their planet has oxygen and nitrogen rather than
hydrogen, under a dozen Earth-atmospheres' pressure. The
temperature is rather high, fifty degrees. I imagine their

world, though of nearly Jovian mass, is so close to its sun that the hydrogen was boiled off, leaving a clear field for evolution similar to Earth's.

"The elephantoid comes from a planet with only about half our gravity. He's the single big fellow with a trunk ending in fingers. He gets by in air too thin for us, which indicates the gravity in his cubicle isn't faked either."

Torrance took a long drink. "The rest all live under pretty terrestroid conditions," he resumed. "For that reason, I wish they were more probable. But actually, except the gorilloids, they seem like long shots. The helmet beasts—"

"What's that?" asked Van Rijn.

"Oh, you remember," said Jeri. "Those eight or nine things like humpbacked turtles, not much bigger than your head. They crawl around on clawed feet, waving little tentacles that end in filaments. They blot up food through those: soupy stuff the machines dump into their trough. They haven't anything like effective hands—the tentacles could only do a few very simple things—but we gave them some time because they do seem to have better developed eyes than parasites usually do."

"Parasites don't evolve intelligence," said Van Rijn. "They got better ways to make a living, by damn. Better make sure the helmet beasts really are parasites—in their home environments—and got no hands tucked under those shells—before you quite write them off. Who else you got?"

"The tiger apes," said Torrance. "Those striped carnivores built something like bears. They spend most of their time on all fours, but they do stand up and walk on their hind legs sometimes, and they do have hands. Clumsy, thumbless ones, with retractable claws, but on all their limbs. Are four hands without thumbs as good as two with? I don't know. I'm too tired to think."

"And that's all, ha?" Van Rijn tilted the bottle to his lips. After a prolonged gurgling he set it down, belched, and blew smoke through his majestic nose. "Who's to try next, if the gorilloids flunk?"

"It better be the caterpiggles, in spite of the air pressure," said Jeri. "Then . . . oh . . . the tentacle centaurs, I suppose. Then maybe the—"

"Horse maneuvers!" Van Rijn's fist struck the table. The bottle and glasses jumped. "How long it takes to catch and check each one? Hours, *nie?* And in between times, takes many more hours to adjust the apparatus and chase out all the hiccups it develops under a new set of conditions. Also, Yamamura will collapse if he can't sleep soon, and who else we got can do this? All the whiles, the forstunken Adderkops get closer. We have not got time for that method! If the gorilloids don't fan out, then only logic will help us. We must deduce from the facts we have, who the Eksers are."

"Go ahead." Torrance drained his glass. "I'm going to take a nap."

Van Rijn purpled. "That's right!" he huffed. "Be like everybody elses. Loaf and play, dance and sing, enjoy yourselfs the liver-long day. Because you always got poor old Nicholas van Rijn there, to heap the work and worry on his back. Oh, dear St. Dismas, why can't you at least make some *one* other person in this whole universe do something useful?"

. . . Torrance was awakened by Yamamura. The gorilloids were not the Eksers. They were color blind and incapable of focusing on the ship's instruments; their brains were small, with nearly the whole mass devoted to purely animal functions. He estimated their intelligence as equal to a dog's.

The captain stood on the bridge of the yacht, because it was a familiar place, and tried to accustom himself to being doomed.

Space had never seemed so beautiful as now. He was not well acquainted with the local constellations, but his trained gaze identified Perseus, Auriga, Taurus, not much distorted since they lay in the direction of Earth. (And of Ramanujan, where gilt towers rose out of mists to catch the first sunlight, blinding against blue Mount Gandhi). A few individuals could also be picked out, ruby Betelgeuse, amber Spica, the pilot stars by which he had steered through his whole working life. Otherwise, the sky was aswarm with small frosty fires, across blackness unclouded and endless. The Milky Way girdled it with cool silver, a nebula glowed faint and green, another galaxy spiraled on the mysterious edge of visibility. He thought less about the planets he had trod, even his own, than about this faring between them which was soon to terminate. For end it would, in a burst of violence too swift to be felt. Better go out thus cleanly when the Adderkops came, than into their dungeons.

He stubbed out his cigarette. Returning, his hand caressed the dear shapes of controls. He knew each switch and knob as well as he knew his own fingers. This ship was his; in a way, himself. Not like that other, whose senseless control board needed a giant and a dwarf, whose emergency switch fell under a mere slap if it wasn't hooked in place, whose—

A light footfall brought him twisting around. Irrationally, so strained was he, his heart flew up within him. When he saw it was Jeri, he eased his muscles, but the pulse continued quick in his blood.

She advanced slowly. The overhead light gleamed on her yellow hair and in the blue of her eyes. But she avoided his glance, and her mouth was not quite steady.

"What brings you here?" he asked. His tone fell even more soft than he had intended.

"Oh . . . the same as you." She stared out the viewscreen. During the time since they captured the alien ship, or it captured them, a red star off the port bow had visibly grown. Now it burned baleful as they passed, a light-year distant. She grimaced and turned her back to it. "Yamamura is readjusting the test apparatus," she said thinly. "No one else knows enough about it to help him, but he has the shakes so bad from exhaustion he can scarcely do the job himself. Old Nick just sits in his suite, smoking and drinking. He's gone through that one bottle already, and started another. I couldn't breathe in there any longer, it was so smoky. And he won't say a word. Except to himself, in Malay or something. I couldn't stand it."

"We may as well wait," said Torrance. "We've done everything we can, till it's time to check a caterpiggle. We'll have to do that spacesuited, in their own cage, and hope they don't all attack us."

She slumped. "Why bother?" she said. "I know the situation as well as you. Even if the caterpiggles are the Eksers, under those conditions we'll need a couple of days to prove it. I doubt if we have that much time left. If we start toward Valhalla two days from now, I'll bet we're detected and run down before we get there. Certainly, if the caterpiggles are only animals too, we'll never get time to test a third species. Why bother?"

"We've nothing else to do," said Torrance.

"Yes, we do. Not this ugly, futile squirming about, like cornered rats. Why can't we accept that we're going to die, and use the time to . . . to be human again?"

Startled, he looked back from the sky to her. "What do you mean?"

Her lashes fluttered downward. "I suppose that would depend on what we each prefer. Maybe you'd want to, well, get your thoughts in order or something."

"How about you?" he asked through his heartbeat.

"I'm not a thinker." She smiled forlornly. "I'm just a shallow sort of person. I'd like to enjoy life while I have it." She half turned from him. "But I can't find anyone I'd like to enjoy it with."

He, or his hands, grabbed her bare shoulders and spun her around to face him. She felt silken under his palms. "Are you sure you can't?" he said roughly. She closed her eyes and stood with face tilted upward, lips half parted. He kissed her. After a second she responded.

After a minute, Nicholas van Rijn appeared in the doorway.

He stood an instant, pipe in hand, gun belted to his waist, before he flung the churchwarden shattering to the deck. "So!" he bellowed.

"Oh!" wailed Jeri.

She disengaged herself. A tide of rage mounted in Torrance. He knotted his fists and started toward Van Rijn.

"So!" repeated the merchant. The bulkheads seemed to quiver with his voice. "By louse-bitten damn, this is a fine thing for me to come on. Satan's tail in a mousetrap! I sit hour by hour sweating my brain to the bone for the sake of your worthless life, and all whiles you, you illegitimate spawn of a snake with dandruff and a cheese mite, here you are making up to my own secretary hired with my own hard-earned money! Gargoyles and *Götterdämmerung!* Down on your knees and beg my pardon, or I mash you up and sell you for dogfood!"

Torrance stopped, a few centimeters from Van Rijn. He was slightly taller than the merchant, if less bulky, and at least thirty years younger. "Get out," he said in a strangled voice.

Van Rijn turned puce and gobbled at him.

"Get out," repeated Torrance. "I'm still the captain of this ship. I'll do what I damned well please, without interference from any loud-mouthed parasite. Get off the bridge, or I'll toss you out on your fat bottom!"

The color faded in Van Rijn's cheeks. He stood motionless for whole seconds. "Well, by damn," he whispered at last. "By damn and death, cubical. He has got the nerve to talk back."

His left fist came about in a roundhouse swing. Torrance blocked it, though the force nearly threw him off his feet. His own left smacked the merchant's stomach, sank a short way into fat, encountered the muscles, and rebounded bruised. Then Van Rijn's right fist clopped. The cosmos exploded around Torrance. He flew up in the air, went over backward, and lay where he fell.

When awareness returned, Van Rijn was cradling his head and offering brandy which a tearful Jeri had fetched.

"Here, boy. Go slow there. A little nip of this, ha? That goes good. There, now you only lost one tooth and we get that fixed at Freya. You can even put it on expense account. There, that makes you feel more happy, *nie?* Now, girl, Jarry, Jelly, whatever your name is, give me that stimpill. Down the hatchworks, boy. And then, upsy-rosy, onto your feet. You should not miss the fun."

One-handed, Van Rijn heaved Torrance erect. The captain leaned a while on the merchant, until the stimpill removed aches and dizziness. Then, huskily through swollen lips, he asked, "What's going on? What d' you mean?"

"Why, I know who the Eksers are. I came to get you, and we fetch them from their cage." Van Rijn nudged Torrance with a great splay thumb and whispered almost as softly as a hurricane, "Don't tell anyone or I have too many fights, but I like a brass-bound nerve like you got. When we get home, I think you transfer off this yacht to command of a trading squadron. How you like that, ha? But come, we still got a damn plenty of work to do."

Torrance followed him in a daze: through the small ship and the tube, into the alien, down a corridor and a ramp to the zoological hold. Van Rijn gestured at the spacemen posted on guard lest the Eksers make a sally. They drew their guns and joined him, their weary slouch jerking to alertness when he stopped before an air lock.

"*Those?*" sputtered Torrance. "But—I thought—"

"You thought what they hoped you would think," said Van Rijn grandly. "The scheme was good. Might have worked, not counting the Adderkops, except that Nicholas van Rijn was here. Now, then. We go in and take them all out, making a good show of our weapons. I hope we need not get too tough with them. I expect not, when we explain by drawings how we understand all their secret. Then they should take us to Valhalla, as we can show by those pretty astronautical diagrams Captain Torrance has already prepared. They will cooperate under threats, as prisoners, at first. But on the voyage, we can use the standard means to establish alimentary communications

. . . no, terror and taxes, I mean rudimentary . . . anyhows, we get the idea across that all humans are not Adderkops and we want to be friends and sell them
things. Hokay? We go!"

He marched through the air lock, scooped up a helmet
beast, and bore it kicking out of its cage.

Torrance didn't have time for anything en route except
his work. First the entry hole in the prize must be sealed,
while supplies and equipment were carried over from the
Hebe G.B. Then the yacht must be cast loose under her
own hyperdrive; in the few hours before her converter
quite burned out, she might draw an Adderkop in chase.
Then the journey commenced, and though the Eksers laid
a course as directed, they must be constantly watched lest
they try some suicidal stunt. Every spare moment must be
devoted to the urgent business of achieving a simple
common language with them. Torrance must also super-
vise his crew, calm their fears, and maintain a detector-
watch for enemy vessels. If any had been detected, the
humans would have gone off hyperdrive and hoped they
could lie low. None were, but the strain was considerable.

Occasionally he slept.

Thus he got no chance to talk to Van Rijn at length. He
assumed the merchant had had a lucky hunch, and let it
go at that.

Until Valhalla was a tiny yellow disc, outshining all
other stars; a League patrol ship closed on them; and,
explanations being made, it gave them escort as they
moved at sublight speed toward Freya.

The patrol captain intimated he'd like to come aboard.
Torrance stalled him. "When we're in orbit, Freeman
Agilik, I'll be delighted. But right now, things are pretty
disorganized. You can understand that, I'm sure."

He switched off the alien telecom he had now learned to
operate. "I'd better go below and clean up," he said.
"Haven't had a bath since we abandoned the yacht. Carry

on, Freeman Lafarge." He hesitated. "And—uh—Freeman Jukh-Barklakh."

Jukh grunted something. The gorilloid was too busy to talk, squatting where a pilot seat should have been, his big hands slapping control plates as he edged the ship into a hyperbolic path. Barklakh, the helmet beast on his shoulders, who had no vocal cords of his own, waved a tentacle before he dipped it into the protective shaftlet to turn a delicate adjustment key. The other tentacle remained buried on its side of the gorilloid's massive neck, drawing nourishment from the bloodstream, receiving sensory impulses, and emitting the motor-nerve commands of a skilled space pilot.

At first the arrangement had looked vampirish to Torrance. But though the ancestors of the helmet beasts might once have been parasites on the ancestors of the gorilloids, they were so no longer. They were symbionts. They supplied the effective eyes and intellect, while the big animals supplied strength and hands. Neither species was good for much without the other; in combination, they were something rather special. Once he got used to the idea, Torrance found the sight of a helmet beast using its claws to climb up a gorilloid no more unpleasant than a man in a historical stereopic mounting a horse. And once the helmet beasts were used to the idea that not all humans were enemies, they showed a positive affection for them.

Doubtless they're thinking what lovely new specimens we can sell them for their zoo, reflected Torrance. He slapped Barklakh on the shell, patted Jukh's fur, and left the bridge.

A sponge bath of sorts and fresh garments took the edge off his weariness. He thought he'd better warn Van Rijn, and knocked at the cabin which the merchant had curtained off as his own.

"Come in," boomed the bass voice. Torrance entered a cubicle blue with smoke. Van Rijn sat on an empty brandy case, one hand holding a cigar, the other holding Jeri, who was snuggled on his lap.

"Well, sit down, sit down," he roared cordially. "You find a bottle somewhere in all those dirty clothes in the corner."

"I stopped by to tell you, sir, we'll have to receive the captain of our escort when we're in orbit around Freya, which'll be soon. Professional courtesy, you know. He's naturally anxious to meet the Eks—uh—the Togru-Kon-Tanakh."

"Hokay, pipe him aboard, lad." Van Rijn scowled. "Oney make him bring his own bottle, and not take too long. I want to land, me, I'm sick of space. I think I'll run barefoot over the soft cool acres and acres of Freya, by damn!"

"Maybe you'd like to change clothes?" hinted Torrance.

"Ooh!" squeaked Jeri, and ran off to the cabin she sometimes occupied. Van Rijn leaned back against the wall, hitched up his sarong and crossed his shaggy legs as he said: "If that captain comes to meet the Eskers, so let him meet the Eksers. I stay comfortable like I am. And I will not entertain him with how I figured out who they were. That I keep exclusive, for sale to what news syndicate bids highest. Understand?"

His eyes grew unsettlingly sharp. Torrance gulped. "Yes, sir."

"Good. Now do sit down, boy. Help me put my story in order. I have not your fine education, I was a poor lonely hardworking old man from I was twelve, so I would need some help making my words as elegant as my logic."

"Logic?" echoed Torrance, puzzled. He tilted the bottle, chiefly because the tobacco haze in here made his eyes smart. "I thought you guessed—"

"What? You know me so little as that? No, no, by damn. Nicholas van Rijn never guesses. I *knew*." He reached for the bottle, took a hefty swig, and added magnanimously, "That is, after Yamamura found the gorilloids alone could not be the peoples we wanted. Then I sat down and uncluttered my brains and thought it all over.

"See, it was simple eliminations. The elephantoid was out right away. Only one of him. Maybe, in emergency, one could pilot this ship through space—but not land it, and pick up wild animals, and care for them, and all else. Also, if somethings go wrong, he is helpless."

Torrance nodded. "I did consider it from the spaceman's angle," he said. "I was inclined to rule out the elephantoid on that ground. But I admit I didn't see the animal-collecting aspect made it altogether impossible that this could be a one-being expedition."

"He was pretty too big anyhow," said Van Rijn. "As for the tiger apes, like you, I never took them serious. Maybe their ancestors was smaller and more biped, but this species is reverting to quadruped again. Animals do not specialize in being everything. Not brains and size and carnivore teeth and cat claws, all to once.

"The caterpiggles looked hokay till I remembered that time you accidental turned on the bestonkered emergency acceleration switch. Unless hooked in place, what such a switch would not be except in special cases, it fell rather easy. So easy that its own weight would make it drop open under three Earth gravities. Or at least there would always be serious danger of this. Also, that shelf you bumped into, they wouldn't build shelves so light on high-gravity planets."

He puffed his cigar back to furnace heat. "Well, so might be the tentacle centaurs," he continued. "Which was bad for us, because hydrogen and oxygen explode. I checked hard through the reports on the ship, hoping I could find something that would eliminate them. And by damn, I did. For this I will give St. Dismas an altar cloth, not too expensive. You see, the Eksers is kind enough to use copper oxide rectifiers, exposed to the air. Copper oxide and hydrogen, at a not very high temperature such as would soon develop from strong electricking, they make water and pure copper. Poof, no more rectifier. So therefore

ergo, this ship was not designed for hydrogen breathers."
He grinned. "You has had so much high scientific education you forgot your freshlyman chemistry."

Torrance snapped his fingers and swore at himself.

"By eliminating, we had the helmet beasts," said Van
Rijn. "Only they could not possible be the builders. True,
they could handle certain tools and controls, like that
buried key; but never all of it. And they are so slow and
small. How could they ever stayed alive long enough to
invent spaceships? Also, animals that little don't got room
for real brains. And neither armored animals nor parasites
ever get much. Nor do they get good eyes. And yet the
helmet beasts seemed to have very good eyes, as near as
we could tell. They looked like human eyes, anyhows.

"I remembered there was both big and little cubbyholes
in these cabins. Maybe bunks for two kinds of sleeper?
And I thought, is the human brain a turtle just because it
is armored in bone? A parasite just because it lives off
blood from other places? Well, maybe some people I could
name but won't, like Juan Harleman of the Venusian Tea
& Coffee Growers, Inc., has parasite turtles for brains. But
not me. So there I was. Q.," said Van Rijn smugly, "E.D."

Hoarse from talking, he picked up the bottle. Torrance
sat a few minutes more, but as the other seemed disin-
clined to conversation, he got up to go.

Jeri met him in the doorway. In a slit and topless blue
gown which fitted like a coat of lacquer, she was a fourth-
order stunblast. Torrance stopped in his tracks. Her gaze
slid slowly across him, as if reluctant to depart.

"Mutant sea-otter coats," murmured Van Rijn dream-
ily. "Martian firegems. An apartment in the Stellar
Towers."

She scampered to him and ran her fingers through his
hair. "Are you comfortable, Nicky, darling?" she purred.
"Can't I do something for you?"

Van Rijn winked at Torrance. "Your technique, that
time on the bridge, I watched and it was lousy," he said

to the captain. "Also, you are not old and fat and lonesome; you have a happy family for yourself."

"Uh—yes," said Torrance. "I do." He let the curtain drop and returned to the bridge.

It is a truism that the structure of a society is basically determined by its technology. Not in an absolute sense—there may be totally different cultures using identical tools—but the tools settle the possibilities: you can't have interstellar trade without spaceships. A race limited to one planet, possessing a high knowledge of mechanics but with all its basic machines of commerce and war requiring a large capital investment, will inevitably tend toward collectivism under one name or another. Free enterprise needs elbow room.

Automation made manufacturing cheap, and the cost of energy nose-dived when the proton converter was invented. Gravity control and the hyperdrive opened a galaxy to exploitation. They also provided a safety valve: a citizen who found his government oppressive could usually emigrate elsewhere, a fact which strengthened the libertarian planets; their influence in turn loosened the bonds of the older world.

Interstellar distances being what they are, and intelligent races all having their own ideas of culture, there was no universal union. Neither was there much war: too destructive, with small chance for either side to escape ruin, and too little to fight about. A species doesn't get to be intelligent without an undue share of built-in ruthlessness, so all was not sweetness and brotherhood—but the balance of power remained fairly stable. And there was a brisk demand for trade goods. Not only did colonies want the luxuries of home, and the home planets want colonial produce, but the old worlds themselves had much to swap.

Under such conditions, an exuberant capitalism was bound to strike root. It was also bound to find mutual interests, to form alliances, and to settle spheres of influence. The powerful companies joined together to squeeze out competition, jack up prices, and generally make the best of a good thing. Governments were limited to a few planetary systems each, at most; they could do little to control their cosmopolitan merchants. One by one, through bribery, coercion, or sheer despair, they gave up the attempt.

Selfishness is a potent force. Governments, officially dedicated to altruism, remained divided; the Polesotechnic League became a supergovernment, sprawling from Canopus to Polaris, drawing its membership from a thousand species. It was a horizontal society, cutting across all political and cultural boundaries. It set its own policies, made its own treaties, established its own bases, fought its own minor wars—and, in the course of milking the Milky Way, did more to spread a truly universal civilization and enforce a lasting *Pax* than all the diplomats in the galaxy.

But it had its troubles.

—Margin of Profit

TERRITORY

Joyce Davisson awoke as if she had been stabbed.

The whistle came again, strong enough to penetrate mortar and metal and insulation, on into her eardrums. She sat up in the dark with a gasp of recognition. When last she heard that wildcat wail, it was in the Chabanda, and it meant that two bands were hunting each other. But then she had been safely aloft in a flitter, armed men on either side of her and a grave Ancient for guide. What she saw and heard came to her amplified by instruments that scanned the ice desert glittering beneath. Those tiger-striped warriors who slew and died were only figures in a screen. She had felt sorry for them, yet somehow they were not quite real: individuals only, whom she had never met, atoms that perished because their world was perishing. Her concern was with the whole.

Now the whistle was against her station.

It couldn't be!

An explosion went *crump*. She heard small things rattle on her desk top and felt her bed shaken. Suddenly the glissandos were louder in her head, and a snarl of drum-

taps accompanied them, a banging on metal and a crashing as objects were knocked off shelves. The attackers
must have blown down the door of the machine section
and swarmed through. Only where could they have gotten
the gunpowder?

Where but in Kusulongo the City?

That meant the Ancients had decided the humans were
better killed. The fear of death went through Joyce in a
wave. It passed on, leaving bewilderment and pain, as if
she were a child struck for no reason. Why had they done
this to her, who came for nothing but to help them?

Feet pounded in the hall just outside the Terrestrialized
section of the dome. The mission's native staff had roused
and were coming out of their quarters with weapons to
hand. She heard savage yells. Then, farther off among
the machines, combat broke loose. Swords clattered, tomahawks cracked on bone, the pistol she had given Uulobu
spoke with an angry snap. But her gang couldn't hold out
long. The attackers had to be Shanga, from the camp in
the oasis just under Kusulongo the Mountain. No other
clan was near, and the Ancients themselves never fought
aggressively. But there were hundreds of male Shanga in
the oasis, while the mission had scarcely two dozen trustworthy t'Kelans.

Heavily armored against exterior conditions, the human
area would not be entered as easily as the outside door of
the machine section had been destroyed. But once the
walls were cracked—

Joyce bounded to her feet. One hand passed by the
main switch plate on its way to her gear rack, and the
lights came on. The narrow, cluttered room, study as well
as sleeping place, looked somehow distorted in that white
glow. Because I'm scared, she realized. I'm caught in a
living nightmare. Nerve and muscle carried on without
her mind. She leaped into the form-fitting Long John
and the heavy fabricord suit. Drawing the skin-thin gloves
over her hands, she connected their wiring to the electric
net woven into the main outfit. Now: kerofoamsoled

boots; air renewal tank and powerpack on the back; pistol and bandolier; pouched belt of iron rations; minicom in breast pocket; vitryl helmet snugged down on the shoulders but faceplate left open for the time being.

Check all fasteners, air system, heat system, everything. The outdoors is lethal on t'Kela. The temperature, on this summer night in the middle latitudes, is about sixty degrees below zero Celsius. The partial pressure of nitrogen will induce narcosis, the ammonia will burn out your lungs. There is no water vapor that your senses can detect; the air will suck you dry. None of these factors differ enough from Earth to kill you instantly. No, aided by an oxygen content barely sufficient to maintain your life, you will savor the process for minutes before you even lose consciousness.

And the Shanga out there, now busily killing your native assistants, have gunpowder to break down these walls.

Joyce whirled about. The others! There was no intercom; two dozen people in one dome didn't need any. She snatched at the door of the room adjoining hers. Nothing happened. "Open up, you idiot!" she heard herself scream above the noise outside. "Come along! We've got to get away—"

A hoarse basso answered through the panels, "What you mean, open up? You locked yourself in, by damn!"

Of course, of course, Joyce's mind fumbled. Her pulse and the swelling racket of battle nearly drowned thought. She'd fastened this door on her own side. During her time with the mission itself, there had never been any reason to do so. But then Nicholas van Rijn landed, and got himself quartered next to her, and she had enough trouble by day fending off his ursine advances . . . She pushed the switch.

The merchant rolled through. Like most Esperancians, Joyce was tall, but she did not come up to his neck. His shoulders filled the doorway and his pot belly strained the fabricord suit that had been issued him. Hung about with survival equipment, he looked still more monstrous than

he had done when snorting his way around the dome in
snuff-stained finery of lace and ruffles. The great hooked
nose jutted from an open helmet, snuffing the air as if for
a scent of blood.

"Hah!" he bawled. Greasy black hair, carefully ring-
leted to shoulder length, swirled as he looked from side to
side; the waxed mustache and goatee threatened every
corner like horns. "What in the name of ten times ten
to the tenth damned souls on a logarithmic spiral to hell
is going on here for fumblydiddles? I thought, me, you had
anyhows the trust of those natives!"

"The others—" Joyce choked. "Come on, let's get together with them."

Van Rijn nodded curtly, so that his several chins quivered, and let her take the lead. Personal rooms in the
human section faced the same corridor, each with a door
opening onto that as well as onto its two neighbors.
Joyce's room happened to be at the end of the row, with
the machine storage section on its farther side. Unmar-
ried and fond of privacy, she had chosen that arrangement
when she first came here. The clubroom was at the hall's
other terminus, around the curve of the dome. As she
emerged from her quarters, Joyce saw door after door
gaping open. The only ones still closed belonged to cham-
bers which nobody occupied, extras built in the antic-
ipation of outside visitors like Van Rijn's party. So
everyone else had already gotten into their suits and down
to the clubroom, the fixed emergency rendezvous. She
broke into a run. Van Rijn's ponderous jog trot made a
small earthquake behind her. Gravity on t'Kela was about
the same as on Earth or Esperance.

The only thing that's the same, Joyce thought wildly.
For an instant she was nearly blinded by the recollection
of her home on the green planet of the star called Pax
—a field billowing with grain, remote blue mountains, the
flag of the sovereign world flying red and gold against a
fleecy sky, and that brave dream which had built the Commonalty.

It roared at her back. The floor heaved underfoot. As she fell, the boom came again, and yet again. The third explosion pierced through. A hammerblow of concussion followed.

Striking the floor, she rolled over. Her head rattled from side to side of her helmet. The taste of blood mixed with smoke in her mouth. She looked back down the corridor through ragged darknesses that came and went before her eyes. The wall at the end, next to her own room, was split and broken. Wild shadowy figures moved in the gloom beyond the twisted structural members.

"They blew it open," she said stupidly.

"Close your helmet," Van Rijn barked. He had already clashed his own faceplate to. The amplifier brought her his gravelly tones, but a dullness would not let them through to her brain.

"They blew it open," she repeated. The thing seemed too strange to be real.

A native leaped into the breach. He could stand Terrestrial air and temperature for a while if he held his breath. And t'Kelan atmosphere, driven by a higher pressure, was already streaming past him. The stocky, striped figure poised in a tension like that of the strung bow he aimed. Huge slit-pupiled eyes glared in the light from the fluoros.

An Esperancian technician came running around the bend of the corridor. "Joyce!" he cried. "Freeman Van Rijn! Where—" The bow twanged. A barbed arrowhead ripped his suit. A moment afterward the air seemed full of arrows, darts, spears, hurled from the murk. Van Rijn threw himself across Joyce. The technician spun on his heel and fled.

Van Rijn's well-worn personal blaster jumped into his fist. He fired from his prone position. The furry shape in the breach tumbled backward. The shadows behind withdrew from sight. But the yell and clatter went on out there.

A first ammoniacal whiff stung Joyce's nostrils. "Pox and pestilence," Van Rijn growled. "You like maybe to breathe that dragon belch?" He rose to his knees and

closed her faceplate. His little black close-set eyes regarded
her narrowly. "So, stunned, makes that the way of it? Well,
hokay, you is a pretty girl with a nice figure and stuff even
if you should not cut your hair so short. Waste not, want
not. I rescue you, ha?"

He dragged her across one shoulder, got up, and backed
wheezily along the hall, his blaster covering the direction
of the hole. "Ugh, ugh," he muttered, "this is not a job
for a poor old fat man who should be at home in his nice
office on Earth with a cigar and maybe a wee glass Genever.
The more so when those misbegotten snouthearts he must
use for help will rob him blind. *Ja,* unscrew his eyeballs
they will, so soon as he isn't looking. But all the factors at
all the trading posts are such gruntbrains that poor Nicholas van Rijn must come out his own selfs, a hundred
light-years in the direction of Orion's bellybutton he must
come, and look for new trading possibilities. Else the
wolves-with-rabies competition tears his Solar Spice &
Liquors Company in shreds and leaves him prostitute in
his old age . . . Ah, here we is. Downsy-daisy."

Joyce shook her head as he eased her to the floor. Full
awareness had come back, and her knees didn't wobble
much. The clubroom door was in front of her. She pushed
the switch. The barrier didn't move. "Locked," she said.

Van Rijn pounded till it shivered. "Open up!" he bellowed. "Thunder and thighbones, what is this farce?"

A native raced around the curve of the hall. Van Rijn
turned. Joyce shoved his blaster aside. "No, that's Uulobu."
The t'Kelan must have exhausted his pistol and thrown it
away, for a tomahawk now dripped in his hand. Three
other autochthones bounded after him, swords and hatch-
ets aloft. Their kilts were decorated with the circle-and-
square insigne of the Shanga clan. "Get them!"

Van Rijn's blaster spat fire. One of the invaders flopped
over. The others whirled to escape. Uulobu yowled and
threw his tomahawk. The keen obsidian edge struck a
Shanga and knocked him down, bleeding. Uulobu yanked

the cord that ran between his weapon and wrist, retrieved the ax, and threw it again to finish the job.

Van Rijn returned to the door. "You termite-bitten cowards, let us in!" As his language got bluer, Joyce realized what must have happened. She pounded his back with her fists, much as he was pounding the door, until he stopped and looked around.

"They wouldn't abandon us," Joyce said. "But they must think we've been killed. When Carlos saw us, back there in the hall, we were both lying on the floor, and there were so many missiles . . . They aren't in the clubroom any longer. They locked the door to delay the enemy while they took a different way to the spaceships."

"Ah, *ja, ja,* must be. But what do we do now? Blast through the door to follow?"

Uulobu spoke in the guttural language of the Kusulongo region. "All of us are slain or fled, sky-female. No more battle. The noise you hear now is the Shanga plundering. If they find us, they will fill us with arrows. Two guns cannot stop that. But I think if we go back among the iron-that-moves, we can slip out that way and around the dome."

"What's he besputtering about?" Van Rijn asked.

Joyce translated. "I think he's right," she added. "Our best chance is to leave through the machine section. It seems deserted for the time being. But we'd better hurry."

"So. Let this pussycat fellow go ahead, then. You stay by me and cover my back, *nie?*"

They trotted back the way they had come. Hoarfrost whitened the walls and made the floor slippery, as water vapor condensed in the t'Kelan cold. The breach into the unlighted machine section gaped like a black mouth. Remotely through walls, Joyce heard ripping, smashing and exultant shouts. The work of years was going to pieces around her. *Why?* she asked in pain, and got no answer.

Uulobu's eyes, more adaptable to dark than any human's, probed among bulky shapes as they entered the storage area. Vehicles were parked here: four ground-cars and as many flitters. In addition, this long chamber housed the specialized equipment of the studies the Esperancians had made, seeking a way to save the planet. Most lay in wreckage on the floor.

An oblong of dim light, up ahead, was the doorway to the outside. Joyce groped forward. Her boot struck something, a fallen instrument. It clanked against something else.

There came a yammer of challenge. The entrance filled with a dozen shapes. They whipped through and lost themselves among shadows and machines before Van Rijn could fire. Uulobu hefted his tomahawk and drew his knife. "Now we must fight for our passage," he said unregretfully.

"Cha-a-a-arge!" Van Rijn led the way at a run. Several t'Kelans closed in on him. Metal and polished stone whirled in the murk. The Earthman's blaster flared. A native screamed. Another native got hold of the gun arm and dragged it downward. Van Rijn tried to shake him loose. The being hung on, though the human clubbed him back and forth against his fellows.

Uulobu joined the ruckus, stabbing and hacking with carnivore glee. Joyce could not do less. She had her own pistol out, a slug-thrower. Something bumped into the muzzle. Fangs and eyes gleamed at her in what light there was. A short spear poised, fully able to pierce her suit. Even so, she had never done anything harder than to pull the trigger. The crack of the gun resounded in her own skull.

Then for a while it was jostling, scrabbling, firing, falling, and wrestling lunacy. Now and again Joyce recognized Uulobu's screech, the battle cry of his Avongo clan. Van Rijn's voice sounded above the din like a trumpeted, "St. Dismas help us! Down with mangy dogs!" Suddenly it was over. The guns had been too much. She lay on the floor, struggling for breath, and heard the last few

Shanga run out. Somewhere a wounded warrior groaned, until Uulobu cut his throat.

"Up with you," Van Rijn ordered between puffs. "We got no time for making rings around the rosies."

Uulobu helped her rise. He was too short to lean on very well, but Van Rijn offered her an arm. They staggered out of the door, into the night.

There was no compound here, only the dome and then t'Kela itself. Overhead glittered unfamiliar constellations. The larger moon was aloft, nearly full, throwing dim coppery light on the ground. West and south stretched a rolling plain, thinly begrown with shrubs not unlike Terrestrial sagebrush in appearance: low, wiry, silvery-leaved. Due north rose the sheer black wall of Kusulongo the Mountain, jagged against the Milky Way. The city carved from its top could be seen only as a glimpse of towers like teeth. Some kilometers eastward, at its foot, ran the sacred Mangivolo River. Joyce could see a red flash of moonlight on liquid ammonia. The trees of that oasis where the Shanga were camped made a blot of shadow. The hills that marched northward from Kusulongo gleamed with ice, an unreal sheen.

"Hurry," Van Rijn grated. "If the other peoples think we are dead, they will raise ship more fast than they can."

His party rounded the dome at the reeling pace of exhaustion. Two tapered cylinders shimmered under the moon, the mission's big cargo vessel and the luxury yacht which had brought Van Rijn and his assistants from Earth. A couple of dead Shanga lay nearby. The night wind ruffled their fur. It had been a fight to reach safety here. Now the ramps were retracted and the air locks shut. As Van Rijn neared, the whine of engines shivered forth.

"Hey!" he roared. "You clabberbrains, wait for me!"

The yacht took off first, hitting the sky like a thunderbolt. The backwash of air bowled Van Rijn over. Then the Esperancian craft got under weigh. The edge of her drive field caught Van Rijn, picked him up, and threw him several meters. He landed with a crash and lay still.

Joyce hurried to him. "Are you all right?" she choked. He was a detestable old oaf, but the horror of being marooned altogether alone seized upon her.

"Oo-oo-oo," he groaned. "St. Dismas, I was going to put a new stained-glass window in your chapel at home. Now I think I will kick in the ones you have got."

Joyce glanced upward. The spaceships flashed like rising stars, and vanished. "They didn't see us," she said numbly.

"Tell me more," Van Rijn snorted.

Uulobu joined them. "The Shanga will have heard," he said. "They will come out here to make sure, and find us. We must escape."

Van Rijn didn't need that translated. Shaking himself gingerly, as if afraid something would drop off, he crawled to his feet and lurched back toward the dome. "We get a flitter, nie?" he said.

"The groundcars are stocked for a much longer period," Joyce answered. "And we'll have to survive until someone comes back here."

"With the pest-riddled planeteezers chasing us all the while," Van Rijn muttered. "Joy forever, unconfined!"

"We go west, we find my people," Uulobu said. "I do not know where the Avongo are, but other clans of the Rokulela Horde must surely be out between the Narrow Land and the Barrens."

They entered the machine section. Joyce stumbled on a body and shuddered. Had she killed that being herself?

The groundcars were long and square-built; the rear four of the eight wheels ran on treads. The accumulators were fully charged, energy reserve enough to drive several thousand rough kilometers and maintain Earth-type conditions inside for a year. There were air recyclers and sufficient food to keep two humans going at least four months. Six bunks, cooking and sanitary facilities, maps, navigation equipment, a radio transceiver, spare parts for survival gear—everything was there. It had to be, when you traveled on a planet like this.

Van Rijn heaved his bulk through the door, which was not locked, and settled himself in the driver's seat. Joyce collapsed beside him. Uulobu entered with uneasy eyes and quivering whiskers. Only the Ancients, among t'Kelans, liked riding inside a vehicle. That was no problem, though, Joyce recalled dully. On field trips, once you had established a terrestroid environment within, your guides and guards rode on top of the car, talking with you by intercom. Thus many kilometers had been covered, and much had been learned, and the plans had been drawn that would save a world . . . and now!

Van Rijn's ham hands moved deftly over the controls. "In my company we use Landmasters," he said. "I like not much these Globetrotters. But sometimes our boys have to—um—borrow one from the competition, so we know how to . . . Ah." The engine purred to life. He moved out through the door, riding the field drive at its one-meter ceiling instead of using the noisier wheels.

But he could have saved his trouble. Other doors in the dome were spewing forth Shanga. There must be a hundred of them, Joyce thought. Van Rijn's lips skinned back from his teeth. "You want to play happy fun games yet, ha?" He switched on the headlights.

A warrior was caught in the glare, dazzled by it so that he stood motionless, etched against blackness. Joyce's eyes went over him, back and forth, as if something visible could explain why he had turned on her. He was a typical t'Kelan of this locality; races varied elsewhere, as on most planets, but no more than among humans.

The stout form was about 150 centimeters tall, heavily steatopygous to store as much liquid as the drying land afforded. Hands and feet were nearly manlike, except for having thick blue nails and only four digits apiece. The fur that covered the whole body was a vivid orange, striped with black, a triangle of white on the chest. The head was round, with pointed ears and enormous yellow cat-eyes, two fleshy tendrils on the forehead, a single nos-tril crossing the broad nose, a lipless mouth full of sharp white teeth framed in restless cilia. This warrior carried a sword—the bladelike horn of a *gondyanga* plus a wooden handle—and a circular shield painted in the colors of the Yagola Horde to which the Shanga clan belonged.

"Beep, beep!" Van Rijn said. He gunned the car forward.

The warrior sprang aside, barely in time. Others tried to attack. Joyce glimpsed one with a bone piston whis-tle in his mouth. The Yagola never used formal battle cries, but advanced to music. A couple of spears clattered against the car sides. Then Van Rijn was through, bound-ing away at a hundred KPH with a comet's tail of dust behind.

"Where we go now?" he demanded. "To yonder town on the mountain? You said they was local big cheeses."

"The Ancients? No!" Joyce stiffened. "They must be the ones who caused this."

"Ha? Why so?"

"I don't know, I don't know. They were so helpful be-fore . . . But it has to be them. They incited . . . No one else could have. W—we never made any enemies among the clans. As soon as we had their biochemistry figured out, we synthesized medicines and—and helped them—" Joyce found suddenly that she could cry. She leaned her helmet in her hands and let go all emotional holds.

"There, there, everything's hunky-dunky," Van Rijn said. He patted her shoulder. "You been a brave girl, as well as pretty. Go on, now, relax, have fun."

T'Kela rotated once in thirty hours and some minutes, with eight degrees of axial tilt. Considerable night re-mained when the car stopped, a hundred kilometers from Kusulongo, and the escapers made camp. Uulobu took a sleeping bag outside while the others Earth-conditioned the interior, shucked their suits, and crawled into bunks. Not even Van Rijn's snores kept Joyce awake.

Dawn roused her. The red sun climbed from the east with a glow like dying coals. Though its apparent diameter was nearly half again that of Sol seen from Earth or Pax from Esperance, the light was dull to human eyes, shadows lay thick in every dip and gash, and the horizon was lost in darkness. The sky was deep purple, cloudless, but filled to the south with the yellow plumes of a dust storm. Closer by, the plain stretched bare, save for sparse gray vegetation, strewn boulders, a coldly shimmering ice field not far nothward. One scavenger foul wheeled overhead on leathery-feathered wings.

Joyce sat up. Her whole body ached. Remembering what had happened made such an emptiness within that she hardly noticed. She wanted to roll over in the blankets, bury her head, and sleep again. Sleep till rescue came, if it ever did.

She made herself rise, go into the bath cubicle, wash, and change into slacks and blouse. With refreshment came hunger. She returned to the main body of the car and began work at the cooker.

The smell of coffee wakened Van Rijn. "Ahhh!" Whalelike in the Long John he hadn't bothered to remove, he wallowed from his bunk and snatched at a cup. "Good girl." He sniffed suspiciously. "But no brandy in it? After our troubles, we need brandy."

"No liquor here," she snapped.

"What?" For a space the merchant could only goggle at her. His jowls turned puce. His mustaches quivered. "Nothings to drink?" he strangled. "Why—why—why, this is extrarageous. Who's responsible? By damn, I see to it he's blacklisted from here to Polaris!"

"We have coffee, tea, powdered milk and fruit juices," Joyce said. "We get water from the ice outside. The chemical unit removes ammonia and other impurities. One does not take up storage space out in the field with liquor, Freeman Van Rijn."

"One does if one is civilized. Let me see your food stocks." He rummaged in the nearest locker. "Dried meat, dried vegetables, dried—Death and destruction!" he wailed. "Not so much as one jar caviar? You want me to crumble away?"

"You might give thanks you're alive."

"Not under this condition. . . . Well, I see somebody had one brain cell still functional and laid in some cigarettes." Van Rijn grabbed a handful and crumbled them into a briar pipe he had stuffed in his bosom. He lit it. Joyce caught a whiff, gagged, and returned to work at the cooker, banging the utensils about with more ferocity than was needful.

Seated at the folding table next to one of the broad windows, Van Rijn crammed porridge down his gape and peered out at the dim landscape. "Whoof, what a place. Like hell with the furnaces on the fritz. How long you been here, anyways?"

"Myself, about a year, as a biotechnician." She decided it was best to humor him. "Of course, the Esperancian mission has been operating for several years."

"*Ja*, that I know. Though I am not sure just how. I was only here a couple of days, you remember, before the trouble started. And any planet is so big and complicated a thing, takes long to understand it even a little. Besides, I had some other work along I must finish before investigating the situation here."

"I admit being puzzled why you came. You deal in spices and things, don't you? But there's nothing here that a human would like. We could digest some of the proteins and other biological compounds—they aren't all poisonous to us—but they lack things we need, like certain amino acids, and they taste awful."

"My company trades with nonhumans too," Van Rijn explained. "Not long ago, my research staff at home came upon the original scientific reports, from the expedition who found this planet fifteen years ago. This galaxy is so big no one can keep track of everything while it happens.

Always we are behind. But anyhows, was mention of some wine that the natives grow."

"Yes, *kungu*. Most of the clans in this hemisphere make it. They raise the berries along with some other plants that provide fiber. Not that they're farmers. A carnivorous race, nomadic except for the Ancients. But they'll seed some ground and come back in time to harvest it."

"Indeed. Well, as you know, the first explorers here was from Throra, which is a pretty similar planet to this only not so ugh. They thought the *kungu* was delicious. They even wanted to take seeds home, but found because of ecology and stuffs, the plant will only grow on this world. Ah-ha, thought Nicholas van Rijn, a chance maybe to build up a very nice little trade with Throra. So because of not having nobody worth trusting that was on Earth to be sent here, I came in my personals to see. Oh, how bitter to be so lonely!" Van Rijn's mouth drooped in an attempt at pathos. One hairy hand stole across the table and closed on Joyce's.

"Here come Uulobu," she exclaimed, pulling free and jumping to her feet. In the very nick of time, bless both his hearts! she thought.

The t'Kelan loped swiftly across the plain. A small animal that he had killed was slung across his shoulders. He was clad differently from the Shanga: in the necklace of fossil shells and the loosely woven blue kilt of his own Avongo clan and Rokulela Horde. A leather pouch at his waist had been filled with liquid.

"I see he found an ammonia well," Joyce chattered, brightly and somewhat frantically, for Van Rijn was edging around the table toward her. "That's what they have those tendrils for, did you know? Sensitive to any trace of ammonia vapor. This world is so dry. Lots of frozen water, of course. You find ice everywhere you go on the planet. Very often hundreds of square kilometers at a stretch. You see, the maximum temperature here is forty below zero Celsius. But ice doesn't do the indigenous life any good. In fact, it's one of the things that are killing this world."

Van Rijn grumped and moved to the window. Uulobu reached the car and said into the intercom, "Sky-female, I have found spoor of hunters passing by, headed west toward the Lubambaru. They can only be Rokulela. I think we can find them without great trouble. Also I have quenched my thirst and gotten meat for my hunger. Now I must offer the Real Ones a share."

"Yes, do so for all of us," Joyce answered.

Uulobu began gathering sticks for a fire. "What he say?" Van Rijn asked. Joyce translated. "So. What use to us, making league with savages out here? We only need to wait for rescue."

"If it comes," Joyce said. She shivered. "When they hear about this at Esperance, they'll send an expedition to try and learn what went wrong. But not knowing we're alive, they may not hurry it enough."

"*My* people will," Van Rijn assured her. "The Polesotechnic League looks after its own, by damn. So soon as word gets to Earth, a warship comes to full investigation. Inside a month."

"Oh, wonderful," Joyce breathed. She went limp and sat down again.

Van Rijn scowled. "Natural," he ruminated, "they cannot search a whole planet. They will know I was at that bestinkered Kusulongo place, and land there. I suppose those Oldsters or Seniles or whatever you call them is sophisticated enough by now in interstellar matters to fob the crew off with some story, if we are not nearby to make contact. So . . . we must remain in their area, in radio range. And radio range has to be pretty close on a red dwarf's planet, where ionosphere characteristicals are poor. But close to our enemies we cannot come so well, if they are whooping after us the whole time. They can dig traps or throw crude bombs or something . . . one way or other, they can kill us even in this car. Ergo, we must establish ourselves as too strong to attack, in the very neighborhood of Kusulongo. This means we need allies. So you have right, we must certain go along to your friend's peoples."

"But you can't make them fight their own race!" Joyce protested.

Van Rijn twirled his mustache. "Can't I just?" he grinned.

"I mean . . . I don't know how, in any practical sense . . . but even if you could, it would be wrong."

"Um-m-m." He regarded her for a while. "You Esperancers is idealists, I hear. Your ancestors settled your planet for a utopian community, and you is still doing good for everybody even at this low date, *nie*? Your mission to help this planet here was for no profit, except it makes you feel good . . ."

"And as a matter of foreign policy," Joyce admitted, under the honesty fetish of her culture. "By assisting other races, we gain their goodwill and persuade them, a little, to look at things our way. If Esperance has enough such friends, we'll be strong and influential without having to maintain armed services."

"From what I see, I doubt very much you ever make nice little vestrymen out of these t'Kelans."

"Well . . . true . . . they *are* out-and-out carnivores. But then, man started as a carnivorous primate, didn't he? And the t'Kelans in this area did achieve an agricultural civilization once, thousands of years ago. That is, grain was raised to feed meat animals. Kusulongo the City is the last remnant. The ice age wiped it out otherwise, leaving savagery—barbarism at most. But given improved conditions, I'm sure the autochthones could recreate it. They'll never have unified nations or anything, as we understand such things. They aren't gregarious enough. But they could develop a world order and adopt machine technology."

"Except, from what you tell me, those snakes squatting on top of the mountain don't want that."

Joyce paused only briefly to wonder how a snake could

squat before she nodded. "I guess so. Though I can't understand why. The Ancients were so helpful at first."

"Means they need to have some sense beaten into their skullbones. Hokay, so for the sake of t'Kela's long-range good, we arrange to do the beating, you and I."

"Well . . . maybe . . . but still . . ."

Van Rijn patted her head. "You just leave the philosophizings to me, little girl," he said smugly. "You only got to cook and look beautiful."

Uulobu had lit his fire and thrown the eyeballs of his kill onto it. His chant to his gods wailed eerily through the car wall. Van Rijn clicked his tongue. "Not so promising materials, that," he said. "You civilize them if you can. I am content to get home unpunctured by very sharp-looking spears, me." He rekindled his pipe and sat down beside her. "To do this, I must understand the situation. Suppose you explain. Some I have heard before, but no harm to repeat." He patted her knee. "I can always admire your lips and things while you talk."

Joyce got up for another cup of coffee and reseated herself at a greater distance. She forced an impersonal tone.

"Well, to begin with, this is a very unusual planet. Not physically. I mean, there's nothing strange about a type M dwarf star having a planet at a distance of half an A.U., with a mass about forty percent greater than Earth's."

"So much? Must be low density, then. Metal-poor."

"Yes. The sun is extremely old. Fewer heavy atoms were available at the time it formed with its planets. T'Kela's overall specific gravity is only four-point-four. It does have some iron and copper, of course . . . As I'm sure you know, life gets started slowly on such worlds. Their suns emit so little ultraviolet, even in flare periods, that the primordial organic materials aren't energized to interact very fast. Nevertheless, life does start eventually, in oceans of liquid ammonia."

"*Ja.* And usual goes on to develop photosynthesis using ammonia and carbon dioxide, to make carbohydrates and the nitrogen that the animals breathe." Van Rijn tapped his sloping forehead. "So much I have even in this dumb old bell. But why does evolution go different now and then, like on here and Throra?"

"Nobody knows for sure. Some catalytic agent, perhaps. In any event, even at low temperatures like these, all the water isn't solid. A certain amount is present in the oceans, as part of the ammonium hydroxide molecule. T'Kelan or Throran plant cells have an analogue of chlorophyl, which does the same job: using gaseous carbon dioxide and 'dissolved' water to get carbohydrates and free oxygen. The animals reverse the process, much as they do on Earth. But the water they release isn't exhaled. It remains in their tissues, loosely held by a specialized molecule. When an organism dies and decays, this water is taken up by plants again. In other words, H-two-O here acts very much like nitrogenous organic material on our kind of planets."

"But the oxygen the plants give off, it attacks ammonia."

"Yes. The process is slow, especially since solid ammonia is denser than the liquid phase. It sinks to the bottom of lakes and oceans, which protects it from the air. Nevertheless, there is a gradual conversion. Through a series of steps, ammonia and oxygen yield free nitrogen and water. The water freezes out. The seas shrink; the air becomes poorer in oxygen; the desert areas grow."

"This I know from Throra. But there a balance was struck. Nitrogen-fixing bacteria evolved and the drying-out was halted, a billion years ago. So they told me once."

"Throra was lucky. It's a somewhat bigger planet than t'Kela, isn't it? Denser atmosphere, therefore more heat conservation. The greenhouse effect on such worlds depends on carbon dioxide and ammonia vapor. Well, several thousand years ago, t'Kela passed a critical point. Just enough ammonia was lost to reduce the greenhouse effect sharply. As the temperature fell, more and more liquid ammonia turned solid and went to the bottom, where it's also quite well protected against melting. This made the climatic change catastrophically sudden. Temperatures dropped so low that now carbon dioxide also turns liquid, or even solid, through part of the year. There's still some vapor in the atmosphere, in equilibrium, but very little. The greenhouse effect *really* dropped off!

"Plant life was gravely affected, as you can imagine. It can't grow without carbon dioxide and ammonia to build its tissues. Animal life died out with it. Areas the size of a Terrestrial continent became utterly barren, almost overnight. I told you that the native agricultural civilization was wiped out. Worse, though, we've learned from geology that the nitrogen-fixing bacteria were destroyed. Completely. They couldn't survive the winter temperatures. So there's no longer any force to balance the oxidation of ammonia. The deserts encroach everywhere, year by year . . . and t'Kela's year is only six-tenths Standard. Evolution has worked hard, adapting life to the change, but the pace is now too rapid for it. We estimate that all higher animals, including the natives, will be extinct within another millennium. In ten thousand years there'll be nothing alive here."

Though she had lived with the realization for months, it still shook Joyce to talk about it. She clamped fingers around her coffee cup till they hurt, stared out the window at drifting dust, and strove not to cry.

Van Rijn blew foul clouds of smoke a while in silence. Finally he rumbled almost gently, "But you have a cure program worked out, *ja?*"

"Oh . . . oh, yes. We do. The research is completed and we were about ready to summon engineers." She found comfort in proceeding.

"The ultimate solution, of course, is to reintroduce nitrogen-fixing bacteria. Our labs have designed an extremely productive strain. It will need a suitable ecology, though, to survive: which means a lot of work with soil chemistry, a microagricultural program. We can hasten everything—begin to show results in a decade—by less subtle methods. In fact, we'll have to do so, or the death process will outrun anything that bacteria can accomplish.

"What we'll do is melt and electrolyze water. The oxygen can be released directly into the air, refreshing it. But some will go to burn local hydrocarbons. T'Kela is rich in petroleum. This burning will generate carbon dioxide, thus strengthening the greenhouse effect. The chemical energy released can also supplement the nuclear power stations we'll install: to do the electrolysis and to energize the combination of hydrogen from water with nitrogen from the atmosphere, recreating ammonia."

"A big expensive job, that," Van Rijn said.

"Enormous. The biggest thing Esperance has yet undertaken. But the plans and estimates have been drawn up. We know we can do it."

"If the natives don't go potshotting engineers for exercise after lunch."

"Yes." Joyce's blond head sank low. "That would make it impossible. We have to have the good will of all of them, everywhere. They'll have to cooperate, work with us and each other, in a planet-wide effort. And Kusulongo the City influences a quarter of the whole world! What have we done? I thought they were our friends . . ."

"Maybe we get some warriors and throw sharp things at them till they appreciate us," Van Rijn suggested.

The car went swiftly, even over irregular ground. An hour or so after it had started again, Uulobu shouted from his seat on top. Through the overhead window the humans saw him lean across his windshield and point. Looking that way, they saw a dust cloud on the northwestern horizon, wider and lower than the one to the south. "Animals being herded," Uulobu said. "Steer thither, sky-folk."

Joyce translated and Van Rijn put the control bar over. "I thought you said they was hunters only," he remarked. "Herds?"

"The Horde people maintain an economy somewhere between that of ancient Mongol cattlekeepers and Amerind bison-chasers," she explained. "They don't actually domesticate the *iziru* or the *bambalo*. They did once, before the glacial era, but now the land couldn't support such a concentration of grazers. The Hordes do still exercise some control over the migrations of the herds, though, cull them, and protect them from predators."

"Um-m-m. What are these Hordes, anyhows?"

"That's hard to describe. No human really understands it. Not that t'Kelan psychology is incomprehensible. But it is nonhuman, and our mission has been so busy gathering planetographical data that we never found time to do psychological studies in depth. Words like 'pride,' 'clan,' and 'Horde' are rough translations of native terms—not very accurate, I'm sure—just as 't'Kela' is an arbitrary name of ours for the whole planet. It means 'this earth' in the Kusulongo language."

"Hokay, no need beating me over this poor old eggnoggin with the too-obvious. I get the idea. But look you, Freelady Davisson . . . I can call you Joyce?" Van Rijn buttered his tones. "We is in the same boat, sink or swim together, except for having no water to do it in, so let us make friends, ha?" He leaned suggestively against her. "You call me Nicky."

She moved aside. "I cannot prevent your addressing me as you wish, Freeman Van Rijn," she said in her frostiest voice.

"Heigh-ho, to be young and not so globulous again! But a lonely old man must swallow his sorrows." Van Rijn sighed like a self-pitying tornado. "Apropos swallowing, *why* is there not so much as one little case beer along? Just one case; one hour or maybe two of sips, to lay the sandstorms in this mummy gullet I got; is that so much to ask, I ask you?"

"Well, there isn't." She pinched her mouth together. They drove on in silence.

Presently they raised the herd: *iziru*, humpbacked and spiketailed, the size of Terran cattle. Those numbered a few thousand, Joyce estimated from previous experience. With vegetation so sparse, they must needs spread across many kilometers.

A couple of natives had spied the car from a distance and came at a gallop. They rode *basai,* which looked not unlike large stocky antelope with tapir faces and a single long horn. The t'Kelans wore kilts similar to Uulobu's, but leather medallions instead of his shell necklace. Van Rijn stopped the car. The natives reined in. They kept weapons ready, a strung bow and a short throwing-spear.

Uulobu jumped off the top and approached them, hands outspread. "Luck in the kill, strength, health, and off-spring!" he wished them in the formal order of import-ance. "I am Tola's son Uulobu, Avongo, Rokulela, now a follower of the sky-folk."

"So I see," the older, grizzled warrior answered coldly. The young one grinned and put his bow away with an elaborate flourish. Uulobu clapped hand to tomahawk. The older being made a somewhat conciliatory gesture and Uulobu relaxed a trifle.

Van Rijn had been watching intently. "Tell me what they say," he ordered. "Everything. Tell me what this means with their weapon foolishness."

"That was an insult the archer offered Uulobu," Joyce explained unhappily. "Disarming before the ceremonies of peace have been completed. It implies that Uulobu isn't formidable enough to be worth worrying about."

"Ah, so. These is rough peoples, them. Not even inside their own Hordes is peace taken for granted, ha? But why should they make nasty at Uulobu? Has he got no prestige from serving you?"

"I'm afraid not. I asked him about it once. He's the only t'Kelan I could ask about such things."

"*Ja?* How come that?"

"He's the closest to a native intimate that any of us in the mission have had. We saved him from a pretty horrible death, you see. We'd just worked out a cure for a local equivalent of tetanus when he caught the disease. So he feels gratitude toward us, as well as having an economic motive. All our regular assistants are—were impoverished, for one reason or another. A drought had killed off too much game in their territory, or they'd been dispossessed, or something like that." Joyce bit her lip. "They . . . they did swear us fealty . . . in the traditional manner . . . and you know how bravely they fought for us. But that was for the sake of their own honor. Uulobu is the only t'Kelan who's shown anything like real affection for humans."

"Odd, when you come here to help them. By damn, but you was a bunch of mackerel heads! You should have begun with depth psychology first of all. That fool planetography could wait . . . Rotten, stinking mackerel, glows blue in the dark . . ." Van Rijn's growl trailed into a mumble. He shook himself and demanded further translation.

"The old one is called Nyaronga, head of this pride," Joyce related. "The other is one of his sons, of course. They belong to the Gangu clan, in the same Horde as Uulobu's Avongo. The formalities have been concluded, and we're invited to share their camp. These people are hospitable enough, in their fashion . . . after bona fides has been established."

The riders dashed off. Uulobu returned. "They must hurry," he reported through the intercom. "The sun will brighten today, and cover is still a goodly ways off. Best we trail well behind so as not to stampede the animals, sky-female." He climbed lithely to the cartop. Joyce passed his words on as Van Rijn got the vehicle started.

"One thing at a time, like the fellow said shaking hands with the octopus," the merchant decided. "You must tell me much, but we begin with going back to why the natives are not so polite to anybody who works for your mission."

"Well . . . as nearly as Uulobu could get it across to me, those who came to us were landless. That is, they'd stopped maintaining themselves in their ancestral hunting grounds. This means a tremendous loss of respectability. Then, too, he confessed—very bashfully—that our helpers' prestige suffered because we never involved them in any fights. The imputation grew up that they were cowards."

"A warlike culture, ha?"

"N-no. That's the paradox. They don't have wars, or even vendettas, in our sense. Fights are very small-scale affairs, though they happen constantly. I suppose that arises from the political organization. Or does it? We've noticed the same thing in remote parts of t'Kela, among altogether different societies from the Horde culture."

"Explain that, if you will be so kind as to make me a little four-decker sandwich while you talk."

Joyce bit back her annoyance and went to the cooker table. "As I said, we never did carry out intensive xenological research, even locally," she told him. "But we do know that the basic social unit is the same everywhere on this world, what we call the pride. It springs from the fact that the sex ratio is about three females to one male. Living together you have the oldest male, his wives, their offspring of subadult age. All males, and females unencumbered with infants, share in hunting, though only males fight other t'Kelans. The small—um—children help out in the work around camp. So do any widows of the leader's father that he's taken in. The size of such a pride ranges up to twenty or so. That's as many as can make a living in an area small enough to cover afoot, on this desert planet."

"I see. The t'Kelan pride answers to the human family. It is just as universal, too, right? I suppose larger units get organized in different ways, depending on the culture."

"Yes. The most backward savages have no organization larger than the pride. But the Kusulongo society, as we call it—the Horde people—the biggest and most advanced culture, spread over half the northern hemisphere—it has a more elaborate superstructure. Ten or twenty prides form what we call a clan, a cooperative group claiming descent from a common male ancestor, controlling a large territory through which they follow the wild herds. The clans in turn are loosely federated into Hordes, each of which holds an annual get-together in some traditional oasis. That's when they trade, socialize, arrange marriages—newly adult males get wives and start new prides—yes, and they adjudicate quarrels, by arbitration or combat, at such times. There's a lot of squabbling among clans, you see, over points of honor or practical matters like ammonia wells. One nearly always marries within one's own Horde; it has its own dress, customs, gods, and so forth."

"No wars between Hordes?" Van Rijn asked.

"No, unless you want to call the terrible things that happen during a *Völkerwanderung* a war. Normally, although individual units from different Hordes may clash, there isn't any organized campaigning. I suppose they simply haven't the economic surplus to maintain armies in the field."

"Um-m-m. I suspect, me, the reason goes deeper than that. When humans want to have wars, by damn, they don't let any little questions of if they can afford it stop them. I doubt t'Kelans would be any different. Um-m-m." Van Rijn's free hand tugged his goatee. "Maybe here is a key that goes tick-a-lock and solves our problem, if we know how to stick it in."

"Well," Joyce said, "the Ancients are also a war preventive. They settle most inter-Horde disputes, among other things."

"Ah, yes, those fellows on the mountain. Tell me about them."

Joyce finished making the sandwich and gave it to Van Rijn. He wolfed it noisily. She sat down and stared out at the scene: brush and boulders and swirling dust under the surly red light, the dark mass of the herd drifting along, a rider who galloped back to head off some stragglers. Far ahead now could be seen the Lubambaru, a range of ice, sharp peaks that shimmered against the crepuscular sky. Faintly to her, above the murmur of the engine, came yelps and the lowing of the animals. The car rocked and bumped; she felt the terrain in her bones.

"The Ancients are survivors of the lost civilization," she said. "They hung on in their city, and kept the arts that were otherwise forgotten. That kind of life doesn't come natural to most t'Kelans. I gather that in the course of thousands of years, those who didn't like it there wandered down to join the nomads, while occasional nomads who thought the city would be congenial went up and were adopted into the group. That would make for some genetic selection. The Ancients are a distinct psychological type. Much more reserved and . . . intellectual, I guess you'd call it . . . than anyone else."

"How they make their living?" Van Rijn asked around a mouthful.

"They provide services and goods for which they are paid in kind. They are scribes, who keep records; physicians; skilled metallurgists; weavers of fine textiles; makers of gunpowder, though they only sell fireworks and keep a few cannon for themselves. They're credited with magical powers, of course, especially because they can predict solar flares."

"And they was friendly until yesterday?"

"In their own aloof, secretive fashion. They must have been plotting the attack on us for some time, though, egging on the Shanga and furnishing the powder to blow open our dome. I still can't imagine why. I'm certain they believed us when we explained how we'd come to save their race from extinction."

"*Ja,* no doubt. Only maybe at first they did not see all the implications." Van Rijn finished eating, belched, picked his teeth with a fingernail, and relapsed into brooding silence. Joyce tried not to be too desperately homesick.

After a long time, Van Rijn smote the control board so that it rang. "By damn!" he bellowed. "It fits together!"

"What?" Joyce sat straight.

"But I still can't see how to use it," he said.

"What do you mean?"

"Shut up, Freelady." He returned to his thoughts. The slow hours passed.

Late in the afternoon, a forest hove into sight. It covered the foothills of the Lubambaru, where an ammonia river coursed thinly and seepage moistened the soil a little. The trees were low and gnarled, with thorny blue trunks and a dense foliage of small greenish-gray leaves. Tall shrubs sprouted in thickets between them. The riders urged their *iziru* into the wood, posted a few pickets to keep watch, and started northward in a compact group, fifteen altogether, plus pack animals and a couple of fuzzy infants in arms. The females were stockier than the males and had snouted faces. Though hairy and homeothermic, the t'Kelans were not mammals; mothers regurgitated food for children who had not yet cut their fangs.

Old Nyaronga led the band, sword rattling at his side, spear in hand and shield on arm, great yellow eyes flickering about the landscape. His half-grown sons flanked the party, arrows nocked to bows. Van Rijn trundled the car in their wake. "They expect trouble?" he asked.

Joyce started from her glum thoughts. "They always expect trouble," she said. "I told you, didn't I, what a quarrelsome race this is—no wars, but so many bloody set-tos. However, their caution is just routine today. Obviously they're going to pitch camp with the other prides of their clan. A herd this size would require all the Gangu to control it."

"You said they was hunters, not herders."

"They are, most of the time. But you see, *iziru* and *bambalo* stampede when the sun flares, and many are so badly sunburned that they die. That must be because they haven't developed protection against ultraviolet since the atmosphere began to change. Big animals with long generations evolve more slowly than small ones, as a rule. The clans can't afford such losses. In a flare season like this, they keep close watch on the herds and force them into areas where there is some shade and where the undergrowth hinders panicky running."

Van Rijn's thumb jerked a scornful gesture at the lowering red disc. "You mean that ember ever puts out enough radiation to hurt a sick butterfly?"

"Not if the butterfly came from Earth. But you know

what type M dwarfs are like. They flare, and when they
do, it can increase their luminosity several hundred percent.
These days on t'Kela, the oxygen content of the air has
been lowered to a point where the ozone layer doesn't
block out as much ultraviolet as it should. Then, too, a
planet like this, with a metal-poor core, has a weak magnetic field. Some of the charged particles from the sun
get through also—adding to an already high cosmic-ray
background. It wouldn't bother you or me, but mankind
evolved to withstand considerably more radiation than is
the norm here."

"*Ja,* I see. Maybe also there not being much radioactive
minerals locally has been a factor. On Throra, the flares
don't bother them. They make festival then. But like you
say, t'Kela is a harder luck world than Throra."

Joyce shivered. "This is a cruel cosmos. That's what
we believe in on Esperance—fighting back against the universe, all beings together."

"Is a very nice philosophy, except that all beings is not
built for it. You is a very sweet child, anyone ever tell you
that?" Van Rijn laid an arm lightly across her shoulder.
She found that she didn't mind greatly, with the gloom
and the brewing star-storm outside.

In another hour they reached the camp site. Humpbacked leather tents had been erected around a flat field
where there was an ammonia spring. Fires burned before
the entrances, tended by the young. Females crouched over
cooking pots, males swaggered about with hands on weapon hilts. The arrival of the car brought everyone to
watch, not running, but strolling up with an elaborate pretense of indifference.

Or is it a pretense? Joyce wondered. She looked out at
the crowd, a couple of hundred unhuman faces, eyes aglow,
spearheads a-gleam, fur rumpled by the whimpering wind,
but scarcely a sound from anyone. They've acted the
same way, she thought, every clan and Horde, everywhere
we encountered them: wild fascination at first, with our
looks and our machines; then a lapse into this cool formal

courtesy, as if we didn't make any real difference for good or ill. They've thanked us, not very warmly, for what favors we could do, and often insisted on making payment, but they've never invited us to their merrymakings or their rites, and sometimes the children throw rocks at us.

Nyaronga barked a command. His pride began pitching their own camp. Gradually the others drifted away.

Van Rijn glanced at the sun. "They sure it flares today?" he asked.

"Oh, yes. If the Ancients have said so, then it will," Joyce assured him. "It isn't hard to predict, if you have smoked glass and a primitive telescope to watch the star surface. The light is so dim that the spots and flare phenomena can easily be observed—unlike a type-G star—and the patterns are very characteristic. Any jackleg astronomer can predict a flare on an M class dwarf, days in advance. Heliograph signals carry the word from Kusulongo to the Hordes."

"I suppose the Old Fogies got inherited empirical knowledge from early times, like the Babylonians knew about planetary movements, *ja* . . . Whoops, speak of the devil, here we go!"

The sun was now not far above the western ridges, which stood black under its swollen disc. A thin curl of clearer red puffed slowly out of it on one side. The *basai* reared and screamed. A roar went through the clansfolk. Males grabbed the animals' bridles and dragged them to a standstill. Females snatched their pots and their young into the tents.

The flame expanded and brightened. Light crept along the shadowy hills and the plains beyond. The sky began to pale. The wind strengthened and threshed in the woods on the edge of camp.

The t'Kelans manhandled their terrified beasts into a long shelter of hides stretched over poles. One bolted. A warrior twirled his lariat, tossed, and brought the creature crashing to earth. Two others helped drag it under cover.

Still the flame from the solar disc waxed and gathered luminosity, minute by minute. It was not yet too brilliant for human eyes to watch unprotected. Joyce saw how a spider web of forces formed and crawled there, drawn in fiery loops. A gout of radiance spurted, died, and was reborn. Though she had seen the spectacle before, she found herself clutching Van Rijn's arm. The merchant stuffed his pipe and blew stolid fumes.

Uulobu got down off the car. Joyce heard him ask Nya-ronga, "May I help you face the angry Real One?"

"No," said the patriarch. "Get in a tent with the females."

Uulobu's teeth gleamed. The fur rose along his back. He unhooked the tomahawk at his waist.

"Don't!" Joyce cried through the intercom. "We are guests!"

For an instant the two t'Kelans glared at each other. Nyaronga's spear was aimed at Uulobu's throat. Then the ₊Avongo sagged a little. "We are guests," he said in a choked voice. "Another time, Nyaronga, I shall talk about this with you."

"You—landless?" The leader checked himself. "Well, peace has been said between us, and there is no time now to unsay it. But we Gangu will defend our own herds and pastures. No help is needed."

Stiff-legged, Uulobu went into the nearest tent. Presently the last *basai* were gotten inside the shelter. Its flap was laced shut, to leave them in soothing darkness.

The flare swelled. It became a ragged sheet of fire next the sun disc, almost as big, pouring out as much light, but of an orange hue. Still it continued to grow, to brighten and yellow. The wind increased.

The heads of prides walked slowly to the center of camp. They formed a ring; the unwed youths made a larger circle around them. Nyaronga himself took forth a brass horn and winded it. Spears were raised aloft, swords and tomahawks shaken. The t'Kelans began to dance, faster and faster as the radiance heightened. Suddenly Nyaronga blew his horn again. A cloud of arrows whistled toward the sun.

"What they doing?" Van Rijn asked. "Exorcising the demon?"

"No," said Joyce. "They don't believe that's possible. They're defying him. They always challenge him to come down and fight. And he's not a devil, by the way, but a god."

Van Rijn nodded. "It fits the pattern," he said, half to himself. "When a god steps out of his rightful job, you don't try to bribe him back, you threaten him. *Ja,* it fits."

The males ended their dance and walked with haughty slowness to their tents. The doorflaps were drawn. The camp lay deserted under the sun.

"Ha!" Van Rijn surged to his feet. "My gear!"

"What?" Joyce stared at him. She had grown so used to wan red light on this day's travel that the hue now pouring in the windows seemed ghastly on his cheeks.

"I want to go outside," Van Rijn told her. "Don't just stand there with tongue unreeled. Get me my suit!"

Joyce found herself obeying him. By the time his gross form was bedecked, the sun was atop the hills and had tripled its radiance. The flare was like a second star, not round but flame-shaped, and nearly white. Long shadows wavered across the world, which had taken on an unnatural brazen tinge. The wind blew dust and dead leaves over the ground, flattened the fires, and shivered the tents till they thundered.

"Now," Van Rijn said, "when I wave, you fix your intercom to full power so they can hear you. Then tell those so-called males to peek out at me if they have the guts." He glared at her. "And be unpolite about it, you understand me?"

Before she could reply he was in the air lock. A minute afterward he had cycled through and was stumping over the field until he stood in the middle of the encampment. Curtly, he signaled.

Joyce wet her lips. What did that idiot think he was

doing? He'd never heard of this planet a month ago. He hadn't been on it a week. Practically all his information about it he had from her, during the past ten or fifteen hours. And he thought he knew how to conduct himself? Why, if he didn't get his fat belly full of whetted iron, it would only be because there was no justice in the universe. Did he think she'd let herself be dragged down with him?

Etched huge and black against the burning sky, Van Rijn jerked his arm again.

Joyce turned the intercom high and said in the vernacular, "Watch, all Gangu who are brave enough! Look upon the male from far places, who stands alone beneath the angered sun!"

Her tones boomed hollowly across the wind. Van Rijn might have nodded. She must squint now to see what he did. That was due to the contrast, not to the illumination per se. It was still only a few percent of what Earth gets. But the flare, with an effective temperature of a million degrees or better, was emitting in frequencies to which her eyes were sensitive. Ultraviolet also, she thought in a corner of her mind: too little to turn a human baby pink, but enough to bring pain or death to these poor dwellers in Hades.

Van Rijn drew his blaster. With great deliberation, he fired several bolts at the star. Their flash and noise seemed puny against the rage up there. Now what—?

"No!" Joyce screamed.

Van Rijn opened his faceplate. He made a show of it, sticking his countenance out of the helmet, into the full light. He danced grotesquely about and thumbed his craggy nose at heaven.

But . . .

The merchant finished with an unrepeatable gesture, closed his helmet again, fired off two more bolts, and stood with folded arms as the sun went under the horizon.

The flare lingered in view for a while, a sheet of ghostly radiance above the trees. Van Rijn walked back to the car through twilight. Joyce let him in. He opened his helmet, wheezing, weeping, and blaspheming in a dozen languages. Frost began to form on his suit.

"Hoo-ee!" he moaned. "And not even a little hundred cc. of whiskey to console my poor old mucky membranes!"

"You could have died," Joyce whispered.

"Oh, no. No. Not that way does Nicholas van Rijn die. At the age of a hundred and fifty, I plan to be shot by an outraged husband. The cold was not too bad, for the short few minutes I could hold my breath. But letting in that ammonia—Terror and taxes!" He waddled to the bath cubicle and splashed his face with loud snortings.

The last flare-light sank. The sky remained hazy with aurora, so that only the brightest stars showed. The most penetrating charged particles from the flare would not arrive for hours; it was safe outside. One by one, the t'Kelans emerged. Fires were poked up, sputtering and glaring in the dark.

Van Rijn came back. "Hokay, I'm set," he said. "Now put on your own suit and come out with me. We got to talk at them."

As she walked into the circle around which stood the swart outlines of the tents, Joyce must push her way through females and young. Their ring closed behind her, and she saw fireglow reflected from their eyes and knew she was hemmed in. It was comforting to have Van Rijn's buk so near and Uulobu's *pad-pad* at her back.

Thin comfort, though, when she looked at the males who waited by the ammonia spring. They had gathered as soon as they saw the humans coming. To her vision they were one shadow, like the night behind them. The fires on either side, that made it almost like day for a t'Kelan, hardly lit the front rank for her. Now and then a flame jumped high in the wind, or sparks went showering, or the dull glow on the smoke was thrown toward the group. Then she saw a barbed obsidian spearhead, a horn sword, an ax or an iron dagger, drawn. The forest soughed beyond the camp and she heard the frightened bawling of *iziru* as they blundered around in the dark. Her mouth went dry.

The fathers of the prides stood in the forefront. Most were fairly young; old age was not common in the desert. Nyaronga seemed to have primacy on that account. He stood, spear in hand, fangs showing in the half-open jaws, tendrils astir. His kilt fluttered in the unrestful air.

Van Rijn came to a halt before him. Joyce made herself stand close and meet Nyaronga's gaze. Uulobu crouched at her feet. A murmur like the sigh before a storm went through the warriors.

But the Earthman waited imperturbable, until at last Nyaronga must break the silence. "Why did you challenge the sun? No sky-one has ever done so before."

Joyce translated, a hurried mumble. Van Rijn puffed himself up visibly, even in his suit. "Tell him," he said, "I came just a short time ago. Tell him the rest of you did not think it was worth your whiles to make defiance, but I did."

"What do you intend to do?" she begged. "A misstep could get us killed."

"True. But if we don't make any steps, we get killed for sure, or starve to death because we don't dare come in radio range of where the rescue ship will be. Not so?" He patted her hand. "Damn these gloves! This would be more fun without. But in all kinds of cases, you trust me, Joyce. Nicholas Van Rijn has not got old and fat on a hundred rough planets, if he was not smart enough to outlive everybody else. Right? Exact. So tell whatever I say to them, and use a sharp tone. Not unforgivable insults, but be snotty, hokay?"

She gulped. "Yes. I don't know why, b-but I will let you take the lead. If—" She suppressed fear and turned to the waiting t'Kelans. "This sky-male with me is not one of my own party," she told them. "He is of my race, but from a more powerful people among them than my people. He wishes me to tell you that though we sky-folk have hitherto not deigned to challenge the sun, he has not thought it was beneath him to do so."

"You never deigned?" rapped someone. "What do you mean by that?"

Joyce improvised. "The brightening of the sun is no menace to our people. We have often said as much. Were none of you here ever among those who asked us?"

Stillness fell again for a moment, until a scarred one-eyed patriarch said grudgingly, "Thus I heard last year, when you—or one like you—were in my pride's country healing sick cubs."

"Well, now you have seen it is true," Joyce replied.

Van Rijn tugged her sleeve. "Hoy, what goes on? Let me talk or else our last chance gets stupided away."

She dared not let herself be angered, but recounted the exchange. He astonished her by answering, "I am sorry, little girl. You was doing just wonderful. Now, though, I have a speech to make. You translate as I finish every sentence, ha?"

He leaned forward and stabbed his index finger just beneath Nyaronga's nose, again and again, as he said harshly, "You ask why I went out under the brightening sun? It was to show you I am not afraid of the fire it makes. I spit on your sun and it sizzles. Maybe it goes out. My sun could eat yours for breakfast and want an encore, by damn! Your little clot hardly gives enough light to see by, not enough to make bogeyman for a baby in my people."

The t'Kelans snarled and edged closer, hefting their weapons. Nyaronga retorted indignantly, "Yes, we have often observed that you sky-folk are nearly blind."

"You ever stood in the light from our cars? You go blind then, *nie?* You could not stand Earth, you. Pop and sputter you'd go, up in a little greasy cloud of smoke."

They were taken aback at that. Nyaronga spat and said, "You must even bundle yourselves against the air."

"You saw me stick my head out in the open. You care to try a whiff of my air for a change? I dare you."

A rumble went through the warriors, half wrath and half unease. Van Rijn chopped contemptuously with one hand. "See? You is more weakling than us."

A big young chieftain stepped forward. His whiskers bristled. "I dare."

"Hokay, I give you a smell." Van Rijn turned to Joyce. "Help me with this bebloodied air unit. I don't want no more of that beetle venom they call air in my helmet."

"But—but—" Helplessly, she obeyed, unscrewing the flush valve on the recycler unit between his shoulders.

"Blow it in his face," Van Rijn commanded.

The warrior stood bowstring taut. Joyce thought of the pain he must endure. She couldn't aim the hose at him. "Move!" Van Rijn barked. She did. Terrestrial atmosphere gushed forth.

The warrior yowled and stumbled back. He rubbed his nose and streaming eyes. For a minute he wobbled around, before he collapsed into the arms of a follower. Joyce refitted the valve as Van Rijn chortled, "I knew it. Too hot, too much oxygen, and especial the water vapor. It makes Throrans sick, so I thought sure it would do the same for these chaps. Tell them he will get well in a little while."

Joyce gave the reassurance. Nyaronga shook himself and said, "I have heard tales about this. Why must you show that poor fool what was known, that you breathe poison?"

"To prove we is just as tough as you, only more so, in a different way," Van Rijn answered through Joyce. "We can whip you to your kennels like small dogs if we choose."

That remark brought a yell. Sharpened stone flashed aloft. Nyaronga raised his arms for silence. It came, in a mutter and a grumble and a deep sigh out of the females watching from darkness. The old chief said with bleak pride, "We know you command weapons we do not. This means you have arts we lack, which has never been denied. It does not mean you are stronger. A t'Kelan is not stronger than a *bambalo* simply because he has a bow to kill it from afar. We are a hunter folk, and you are not, whatever your weapons."

"Tell him," Van Rijn said, "that I will fight their most

powerful man barehanded. Since I must wear this suit
that protects from his bite, he can use armaments. They
will go through fabricord, so it is fair, *nie?*"

"He'll kill you," Joyce protested.

Van Rijn leered. "If so, I die for the most beautifullest
lady on this planet." His voice dropped. "Maybe then you
is sorry you was not more kind to a nice old man when
you could be."

"I won't!"

"You will, by damn!" He seized her wrist so strongly
that she winced. "I know what I am making, you got me?"

Numbly, she conveyed the challenge. Van Rijn drew his
blaster and threw it at Nyaronga's feet. "If I lose, the win-
ner can keep this," he said.

That fetched them. A dozen wild young males leaped
forth, shouting, into the firelight. Nyaronga roared and
cuffed them into order. He glared from one to another
and jerked his spear at an individual. "This is my own
son Kusalu. Let him defend the honor of pride and clan."

The t'Kelan was overtopped by Van Rijn, but was almost as broad. Muscles moved snakishly under his fur. His
fangs glistened as he slid forward, tomahawk in right
hand, iron dagger in left. The other males fanned out,
making a wide circle of eyes and poised weapons. Uulobu
drew Joyce aside. His grasp trembled on her arm. "Could
I but fight him myself," he whispered.

While Kusalu glided about Van Rijn turned, ponderous
as a planet. His arms hung apelike from hunched shoulders. The fires tinged his crude features where they jutted
within the helmet. "Nya-a-ah," he said.

Kusalu cursed and threw the tomahawk with splin-
tering force. Van Rijn's left hand moved at an impossible
speed. He caught the weapon in mid air and threw himself
backward. The thong tautened. Kusalu went forward on
his face. Van Rijn plunged to the attack.

Kusalu rolled over and bounced to his feet in time. His
blade flashed. Van Rijn blocked it with his right wrist. The
Earthman's left hand took a hitch in the thong and

yanked again. Kusalu went to one knee. Van Rijn twisted
that arm around behind his back. Every t'Kelan screamed.

Kusalu slashed the thong across. Spitting, he leaped
erect again and pounced. Van Rijn gave him an expert
kick in the belly, withdrawing the foot before it could be
seized. Kusalu lurched. Van Rijn closed in with a karate
chop to the side of the neck.

Kusalu staggered but remained up. Van Rijn barely
ducked the rip of the knife. He retreated. Kusalu stood a
moment regaining his wind. Then he moved in one
blur.

Things happened. Kusalu was grabbed as he charged
and sent flailing over Van Rijn's shoulder. He hit ground
with a thump. Van Rijn waited. Kusalu still had the dagger. He rose and stalked near. Blood ran from his nostril.

"*Là ci darem la mano,*" sang Van Rijn. As Kusalu prepared to smite, the Earthman got a grip on his right arm,
whirled him around, and pinned him.

Kusalu squalled. Van Rijn ground a knee in his back.
"You say, 'Uncle?' " he panted.

"He'll die first," Joyce wailed.

"Hokay, we do it hard fashion." Van Rijn forced the
knife loose and kicked it aside. He let Kusalu go. But the
t'Kelan had scarcely raised himself when a gauntleted
fist smashed into his stomach. He reeled. Van Rijn pushed
in relentlessly, blow after blow, until the warrior sank.

The merchant stood aside. Joyce stared at him with
horror. "Is all in order," he calmed her. "I did not damage
him permanent."

Nyaronga helped his son climb back up. Two others led
Kusalu away. A low keening went among the massed
t'Kelans. It was like nothing Joyce had ever heard before.

Van Rijn and Nyaronga confronted each other. The
native said very slowly, "You have proven yourself, sky-
male. For a landless one, you fight well, and it was good of
you not to slay him."

Joyce translated between sobs. Van Rijn answered, "Say
I did not kill that young buck because there is no need.

Then say I have plenty territory of my own." He pointed upward, where stars glistened in the windy, hazy sky. "Tell him there is my hunting grounds, by damn."

When he had digested this, Nyaronga asked almost plaintively, "But what does he wish in our land? What is his gain?"

"We came to help—" Joyce stopped herself and put the question to Van Rijn.

"Ha!" the Earthman gloated. "Now we talk about turkeys." He squatted near a fire. The pride fathers joined him; their sons pressed close to clisten. Uulobu breathed happily, "We are taken as friends."

"I do not come to rob your land or game," Van Rijn said in an oleaginous tone. "No, only to make deals, with good profit on both sides. Surely these folks trade with each other. They could not have so much stuffs as they do otherwise."

"Oh, yes, of course." Joyce settled weakly beside him. "And their relationship to the city is essentially quid pro quo, as I told you before."

"Then they will understand bargains being struck. So tell them those Gaffers on the mountain has got jealous of us. Tell them they sicced the Shanga onto our camp. The whole truths, not varnished more than needful."

"What? But I thought—I mean, didn't you want to give them the impression that we're actually powerful? Should we admit we're refugees?"

"Well, say we has had to make a . . . what do the military communiqués say when you has got your pants beaten off? . . . an orderly rearward advance for strategic reasons, to previously prepared positions."

Joyce did. Tendrils rose on the native heads, pupils narrowed, and hands raised weapons anew. Nyaronga asked dubiously, "Do you wish shelter among us?"

"No," said Van Rijn. "Tell him we is come to warn them, because if they get wiped out we can make no nice deals with profit. Tell them the Shanga now has your guns from the dome, and will move with their fellow clans into Rokulela territory."

Joyce wondered if she had heard aright. "But we don't . . . we didn't . . . we brought no weapons except a few personal sidearms. And everybody must have taken his own away with him in the retreat."

"Do they know that, these peoples?"

"Why . . . well . . . would they believe you?"

"My good pretty blonde with curves in all the right places, I give you Nicholas van Rijn's promise they would not believe anything else."

Haltingly, she spoke the lie. The reaction was horrible. They boiled throughout the camp, leaped about, brandished their spears, and ululated like wolves. Nyaronga alone sat still, but his fur stood on end.

"Is this indeed so?" he demanded. It came as a whisper through the noise.

"Why else would the Shanga attack us, with help from the Ancients?" Van Rijn countered.

"You know very well why," Joyce said. "The Ancients bribed them, played on their superstitions, and probably offered them our metal to make knives from."

"*Ja*, no doubt, but you give this old devil here my rhetorical just the way I said it. Ask him does it not make sense, that the Shanga would act for the sake of blasters and slugthrowers, once the Geezers put them up to it and supplied gunpowder? Then tell him this means the Graybeards must be on the side of the Shanga's own Horde . . . what's they called, now?"

"The Yagola."

"So. Tell him that things you overheard give you good reason to believe the Shanga clan will put themselves at the head of the Yagola to move west and push the Rokulela out of this fine country."

Nyaronga and the others, who fell into an ominous quiet as Joyce spoke, had no trouble grasping the concept. As she had told Van Rijn, war was not a t'Kelan institution. But she was not conveying the idea of a full-dress war—

rather, a *Völkerwanderung* into new hunting grounds. And such things were frequent enough on this dying planet. When a region turned utterly barren, its inhabitants must displace someone else, or die in the attempt.

The difference now was that the Yagola were not starved out of their homes. They were alleged to be anticipating that eventuality, plotting to grab off more land with their stolen firearms to give them absolute superiority.

"I had not thought them such monsters," Nyaronga said.

"They aren't," Joyce protested in Anglic to Van Rijn. "You're maligning them so horribly that—that—"

"Well, well, all's fair in love and propaganda," he said. "Propose to Nyaronga that we all return to Kusulonga, collecting reinforcements as we go, to see for ourselves if this business really is true and use numerical advantage while we have still got it."

"You *are* going to set them at each other's throats! I won't be party to any such thing. I'll die first."

"Look, sweet potato, nobody has got killed yet. Maybe nobody has to be. I can explain later. But for now, we have got to strike while the fat is in the fire. They is wonderful excited. Don't give them a chance to cool off till they has positive decided to march." The man laid a hand on his heart. "You think old, short of breath, comfort-loving, cowardly Nicholas van Rijn wants to fight a war? You think again. A formfitting chair, a tall cool drink, a Venusian cigar, *Eine Kleine Nachtmusik* on the taper, aboard his ketch while he sails with a bunch of dancing girls down Sunda Straits, that is only which he wants. Is that much to ask? Be like your own kind, gentle selfs and help me stir them up to fight."

Trapped in her own bewilderment, she followed his lead. That same night, riders went out bearing messages to such other Rokulela clans as were known to be within reach.

The first progress eastward was in darkness, to avoid the still flaring sun. Almost every male, grown or half-grown, rode along, leaving females and young behind in camp. They wore flowing robes and burnooses, their *basai* were blanketed, against the fierce itch that attacked exposed t'Kelan skin during such periods. Most of the charged particles from the star struck the planet's day side, but there was enough magnetic field to bring some around to the opposite hemisphere. Even so, the party made surprisingly good speed. Peering from the car windows, Joyce glimpsed them under the two moons, shadowy shapeless forms that slipped over the harsh terrain, an occasional flash of spearheads. Through the engine's low voice she heard them calling to each other, and the deep earth-mutter of unshod hoofs.

"You see," Van Rijn lectured, "I am not on this world long, but I been on a lot of others, and read reports about many more. In my line of business this is needful. They always make parallels. I got enough clues about these t'Kelans to guess the basic pattern of their minds, from analogizings. You Esperancers, on this other hand, has not had so much experience. Like most colonies, you is too isolated from the galactic mainstream to keep *au courant* with things, like for instance the modern explorer techniques. That was obvious from the fact you did not make depth psychology studies the very first thing, but instead took what you found at face valuation. Never do that, Joyce. Always bite the coin that feeds you, for this is a hard and wicked universe."

"You seem to know what you're about, Nick," she admitted. He beamed and raised her hand to his lips. She made some confused noise about heating coffee and retreated. She didn't want to hurt his feelings; he really was an old dear, under that crust of his.

When she came back to the front seat, placing herself out of his reach, she said, "Well, tell me, what pattern did you deduce? How do their minds work?"

"You assumed they was like warlike human primitives, in early days on Earth," he said. "On the topside, that worked hokay. They is intelligent, with language; they can reason and talk with you; this made them seem easy understood. What you forgot, I think, me, was conscious intelligence is only a small part of the whole selfness. All it does is help us get what we want. But the wanting itself —food, shelter, sex, everything—our motives—they come from deeper down. There is no logical reason even to stay alive. But instinct says to, so we want to. And instinct comes from very old evolution. We was animals long before we became thinkers and, uh—" Van Rijn's beady eyes rolled piously ceilingward—" and was given souls. You got to think how a race evolved before you can take them . . . I mean understand them.

"Now humans, the experts tell me, got started way back when, as ground apes that turned carnivore when the forests shrank up in Africa for lots of megayears. This is when they started to walking erect the whole time, and grew hands fully developed to make weapons because they had not claws and teeth like lions. Hokay, so we is a mean lot, we Homo Sapienses, with killer instincts. But not exclusive. We is still omnivores who can even survive on Brussels sprouts if we got to. Pfui! But we can. Our ancestors been peaceful nutpluckers and living off each other's fleas a long, longer time than they was hunters. It shows.

"The t'Kelans, on the other side, has been carnivores since they was still four-footers. Not very good carnivores. Unspecialized, with no claws and pretty weak biting apparatus even if it is stronger than humans'. That is why they also developed hands and made tools, which led to them getting big brains. Nevertheleast, they have no vegetarian whatsolutely in their ancestors, as we do. And they have much powerfuller killing instincts than us. And is not so gregarious. Carnivores can't be. You get a big concentration of hunters in one spot, and by damn, the game goes away. Is that coffee ready?"

"I think so." Joyce fetched it. Van Rijn slurped it down, disregarding a temperature that would have taken the skin off her palate, steering with one bare splay foot as he drank.

"I begin to see," she said with growing excitement. "That's why they never developed true nations or fought real wars. Big organizations are completely artificial things to them, commanding no loyalty. You don't fight or die for a Horde, any more than a human would fight for . . . for his bridge club."

"Um-m-m, I have known some mighty bloodshot looks across bridge tables. But *ja,* you get the idea. The pride is a natural thing here, like the human family. The clan, with blood ties, is only one step removed. It can excite t'Kelans as much, maybe, as his country can excite a man. But Hordes? *Nie.* An arrangement of convenience only.

"Not that pride and clan is loving-kindness and sugar candy. Humans make family squabbles and civil wars. T'Kelans have still stronger fighting instincts than us. Lots of arguments and bloodshed. But only on a small scale, and not taken too serious. You said to me, is no vendettas here. That means somebody killing somebody else is not thought to have done anything bad. In fact, whoever does not fight—male, anyhow—strikes them as unnatural, like less than normal."

"Is . . . that why they never warmed up to us? To the Esperancian mission, I mean?"

"Partly. Not that you was expected to fight at any specific time. Nobody went out to pick a quarrel when you gave no offense and was even useful. But your behavior taken in one lump added up to a thing they couldn't understand. They figured there was something wrong with you, and felt a goodly natured contempt. I had to prove I was tough as they or tougher. That satisfied their instincts, which then went to sleep and let them listen to me with respects."

Van Rijn put down his empty cup and took out his pipe. "Another thing you lacked was territory," he said. "Animals on Earth, too, has an instinct to stake out and defend a piece of ground for themselves. Humans do. But for carnivores this instinct has got to be very, very, very powerful, because if they get driven away from where the game is, they can't survive on roots and berries. They die.

"You saw yourselfs how those natives what could not maintain a place in their ancestral hunting grounds but went to you instead was looked downwards on. You Esperancers only had a dome on some worthless nibble of land. Then you went around preaching how you had no designs on anybody's country. Ha! They had to believe you was either lying—maybe that is one reason the Shanga attacked you—or else was abnormal weaklings."

"But couldn't they understand?" Joyce asked. "Did they expect us, who didn't even look like them, to think the same way as they do?"

"Sophisticated, civilized t'Kelans could have caught the idea," Van Rijn said. "However, you was dealing with naïve barbarians."

"Except the Ancients. I'm sure they realize—"

"Maybe so. Quite possible. But you made a deadly threat to them. Could you not see? They has been the scribes, doctors, high-grade artisans, sun experts, for ages and ages. You come in and start doing the same as them, only much better. What you expect them to do? Kiss your foots? Kiss any part of your anatomy? Not them! They is carnivores, too. They fight back."

"But we never meant to displace them!"

"Remember," Van Rijn said, wagging his pipe stem at her, "reason is just the lackey for instinct. The Gaffers is more subtle than anybody elses. They can sit still in one place, between walls. They do not hunt. They do not claim thousands of square kilometers for themselves. But does this mean they have no instinct of territoriality? Ha! Not bloody likely! They has only sublimed it. Their work, *that* is their territory—and you moved in on it!"

Joyce sat numbly, staring out into night. Time passed before she could protest. "But we explained to them—I'm sure they understood—we explained this planet will die without our help."

"*Ja, ja.* But a naturally born fighter has less fear of death than other kinds animals. Besides, the death was scheduled for a thousand years from now, did you not say? That is too long a time to feel with emotions. Your own threat to them was real, here and now."

Van Rijn lit his pipe. "Also," he continued around the mouthpiece, "your gabbing about planet-wide cooperation did not sit so well. I doubt they could really comprehend it. Carnivores don't make cooperations except on the most teensy scale. It isn't practical for them. They haven't got such instincts. The Hordes—which, remember, is not nations in any sense—they could never get what you was talking about, I bet. Altruism is outside their mental horizontals. It only made them suspicious of you. The Ancients maybe had some vague notion of your motives, but didn't share them in the littlest. You can't organize these peoples. Sooner will you build a carousel on Saturn's rings. It does not let itself be done."

"You've organized them to fight!" she exclaimed in her anguish.

"No. Only given them a common purpose for this time being. They believed what I said about weapons left in the dome. With minds like that, they find it much the easiest thing to believe. Of course you had an arsenal—everybody does. Of course you would have used it if you got the chance—anybody would. Ergo, you never got the chance; the Shanga captured it too fast. The rest of the story, the Yagola plot against the Rokulela, is at least logical enough to their minds that they had better investigate it good."

"But what are you going to make them do?" She couldn't hold back the tears any longer. "Storm the mountain? They can't get along without the Ancients."

"Sure, they can, if humans substitute."

"B-b-but—but—no, we can't, we mustn't—"

"Maybe we don't have to," Van Rijn said. "I got to play by my ear of tinned cauliflower when we arrive. We will see." He laid his pipe aside. "There, there, now, don't be so sad. But go ahead and cry if you want. Papa Nicky will dry your eyes and blow your nose." He offered her the curve of his arm. She crept into it, buried her face against his side, and wept herself to sleep.

Kusulongo the Mountain rose monstrous from the plain, cliff upon gloomy cliff, with talus slopes and glaciers between, until the spires carved from its top stood ragged across the sun-disc. Joyce had seldom felt the cold and murk of this world as she did now, riding up the path to the city on a horned animal that must be blanketed against the human warmth of her suit. The wind went shrieking through the empty dark sky, around the crags, to buffet her like fists and snap the banner which Uulobu carried on a lance as he rode ahead. Glancing back, down a dizzying sweep of stone, she saw Nyaronga and the half-dozen other chiefs who had been allowed to come with the party. Their cloaks streamed about them; spears rose and fell with the gait of their mounts; the color of their fur was lost in this dreary light, but she thought she made out the grimness on their faces. Immensely far below, at the mountain's foot, lay their followers, five hundred armed and angry Rokulela. But they were hidden by dusk, and if she died on the heights they could give her no more than a vengeance she didn't want.

She shuddered and edged her *basai* close to the one which puffed and groaned beneath Van Rijn's weight. Their knees touched. "At least we have some company," she said, knowing the remark was moronic but driven to say anything that might drown out the wind. "Thank God the flare died away so fast."

"*Ja,* we made good time," the merchant said. "Only three days from the Lubambaru to here, that's quicker than I forewaited. And lots of allies picked up."

She harked back wistfully to the trek. Van Rijn had spent the time being amusing, and had succeeded better than she would have expected. But then they arrived, and the

Shanga scrambled up the mountain one jump ahead of
the Rokulela charge; the attackers withdrew, unwilling
to face cannon if there was a chance of avoiding it; a parley was agreed on; and she couldn't imagine how it might
end other than in blood. The Ancients might let her
group go down again unhurt, as they'd promised—or might
not—but, however that went, before sundown many warriors would lie broken for the carrion fowl. Oh, yes, she
admitted to herself, I'm also afraid of what will happen
to me, if I should get back alive to Esperance. Instigating
combat! Ten years' corrective detention if I'm lucky . . .
unless I run away with Nick and never see home again,
never, never—But to make those glad young hunters die!

She jerked her reins, half minded to flee down the trail
and into the desert. The beast skittered under her. Van
Rijn caught her by the shoulder. "Calm, there, if you
please," he growled. "We has got to outbluff them upstairs.
They will be a Satan's lot harder to diddle than the barbarians was."

"Can we?" she pleaded. "They can defend every ap-
proach. They're stocked for a long siege, I'm certain, longer
than . . . than we could maintain."

"If we bottle them for a month, is enough. For then
comes the League ship."

"But they can send for help, too. Use the heliographs."
She pointed to one of the skeletal towers above. Its mirror
shimmered dully in the red luminance. Only a t'Kelan
could see the others, spaced out in several directions across
the plains and hills. "Or messengers can slip between our
lines—we'd be spread so terribly thin—they could raise the
whole Yagola Horde against us."

"Maybe so, maybe not. We see. Now peep down and let
me think."

They jogged on in silence, except for the wind. After
an hour they came to a wall built across the trail. Impass-
able slopes of detritus stretched on either side. The arch-
way held two primitive cannon. Four members of the city
garrison poised there, torches flickering near the fuses.

Guards in leather helmets and corselets, armed with bows and pikes, stood atop the wall. The iron gleamed through the shadows.

Uulobu rode forth, cocky in the respect he had newly won from the clans. "Let pass the mighty sky-folk who have condescended to speak with your patriarchs," he demanded.

"Hmpf!" snorted the captain of the post. "When have the sky-folk ever had the spirit of a gutted *yangulu?*"

"They have always had the spirit of a *makovolo* in a rage," Uulobu said. He ran a thumb along the edge of his dagger. "If you wish proof, consider who dared cage the Ancients on their own mountain."

The warrior made a flustered noise, collected himself, and stated loudly, "You may pass then, and be safe as long as the peace between us is not unsaid."

"No more fiddlydoodles there," Van Rijn rapped. "We want by, or we take your popguns and stuff them in a place they do not usually go." Joyce forebore to interpret. Nick had so many good qualities; if only he could overcome that vulgarity! But he had had a hard life, poor thing. No one had ever really taken him in hand. . . . Van Rijn rode straight between the cannon and on up the path.

It debouched on a broad terrace before the city wall. Other guns frowned from the approaches. Two score warriors paced their rounds with more discipline than was known in the Hordes. Joyce's eyes went to the three shapes in the portal. They wore plain white robes, and fur was grizzled with age. But their gaze was arrogant on the newcomers.

She hesitated. "I . . . this is the chief scribe—" she began.

"No introduction to secretaries and office boys," Van Rijn said. "We go straight to the boss."

Joyce moistened her lips and told them: "The head of the sky-folk demands immediate parley."

"So be it," said one Ancient without tone. "But you must leave your arms here."

Nyaronga bared his teeth. "There is no help for it," Joyce reminded him. "You know as well as I, by the law of the fathers, none but Ancients and warriors born in the city may go through this gate with weapons." Her own holster and Van Rijn's were already empty.

She could almost see the heart sink in the Rokulela, and remembered what the Earthman had said about instinct. Disarming a t'Kelan was a symbolic emasculation. They put a bold face on it, clattering their implements down and dismounting to stride with stiff backs at Van Rijn's heels. But she noticed how their eyes flickered about, like those of trapped animals, when they passed the gateway.

Kusulongo the City rose in square tiers, black and massive under the watchtowers. The streets were narrow guts twisting between, full of wind and the noise of hammering from the metalsmiths' quarters. Dwellers by birthright stood aside as the barbarians passed, drawing their robes about them as if to avoid contact. The three councillors said no word; stillness fell everywhere as they walked deeper into the citadel, until Joyce wanted to scream.

At the middle of the city stood a block full twenty meters high, windowless, only the door and the ventholes opening to air. Guards hoisted their swords and hissed in salute as the hierarchs went through the entrance. Joyce heard a small groan at her back. The Rokulela followed the humans inside, down a winding hall, but she didn't think they would be of much use. The torchlit cave at the end was cleverly designed to sap a hunter's nerve.

Six white-robed oldsters were seated on a semicircular dais. The wall behind them carried a mosaic, vivid even in this fluttering dimness, of the sun as it flared. Nyaronga's breath sucked between his teeth. He had just been reminded of the Ancients' power. True, Joyce told herself, he knew the humans could take over the same functions. But immemorial habit is not easily broken.

Their guides sat down too. The newcomers remained standing. Silence thickened. Joyce swallowed several times and said, "I speak for Nicholas van Rijn, patriarch of the sky-folk, who has leagued himself with the Rokulela clans. We come to demand justice."

"Here there is justice," the gaunt male at the center of the dais replied. "I, Oluba's son Akulo, Ancient-born, chief in council, speak for Kusulongo the City. Why have you borne a spear against us?"

"Ha!" snorted Van Rijn when it had been conveyed to him. "Ask that old hippopotamus why he started these troubles in the first place."

"You mean hypocrite," Joyce said automatically.

"I mean what I mean. Come on, now. I know very well why he has, but let us hear what ways he covers up."

Joyce put the question. Akulo curled his tendrils, a gesture of skepticism, and murmured, "This is strange. Never have the Ancients taken part in quarrels below the mountains. When you attacked the Shanga, we gave them refuge, but such is old custom. We will gladly hear your dispute with them and arrange a fair settlement, but this is no fight of ours."

Joyce anticipated Van Rijn by snapping in an upsurge of indignation. "They blew down our walls. Who could have supplied them the means but yourselves?"

"Ah, yes." Akulo stroked his whiskers. "I understand your thinking, sky-female. It is very natural. Well, as this council intended to explain should other carriers of your people arrive here and accuse us, we do sell fireworks for magic and celebration. The Shanga bought a large quantity from us. We did not ask why. No rule controls how much may be bought at a time. They must have emptied the powder out themselves, to use against you."

"What's he say?" Van Rijn demanded.

Joyce explained. Nyaronga muttered—it took courage with the Ancients listening—"No doubt the Shanga pridefathers will support that tale. An untruth is a low price for weapons like yours."

"What weapons speak you of?" a councillor interrupted.

"The arsenal the sky-folk had, which the Shanga captured for use against my own Horde," Nyaronga spat. His mouth curled upward. "So much for the disinterested-ness of the Ancients."

"But—No!" Akulo leaned forward, his voice not quite as smooth as before. "It is true that Kusulongo the City did nothing to discourage an assault on the sky-ones' camp. They are weak and bloodless—legitimate prey. More, they were causing unrest among the clans, undermining the ways of the fathers—"

"Ways off which Kusulongo the City grew fat," Joyce put in.

Akulo scowled at her but continued addressing Nyaronga. "By their attack, the Shanga did win a rich plunder of metal. They will have many good knives. But that is not enough addition to their power that they could ever invade new lands when desperation does not lash them. We thought of that too, here on the mountain, and did not wish to see it happen. The concern of the Ancients was ever to preserve a fitting balance of things. If the sky-folk went away, that balance would actually be restored which they endangered. A little extra metal in Yagola hands would not upset it anew. The sky-folk were never seen to carry any but a few hand-weapons. Those they took with them when they fled. There never was an armory in the dome for the Shanga to seize. Your fear was for nothing, you Rokulela."

Joyce had been translating for Van Rijn *sotto voce*. He nodded. "Hokay. Now tell them what I said you should."

I've gone too far to retreat, she realized desolately. "But we did have weapons in reserve!" she blurted. "Many of them, hundreds, whole boxes full, that we did not get a chance to use before the attack drove us outside."

Silence cracked down. The councillors stared at her in horror. Torch flames jumped and shadows chased each other across the walls. The Rokulela chiefs watched with a stern satisfaction that put some self-confidence back into them.

Finally Akulo stuttered, "B-b-but you said—I asked you

once myself, and you denied having—having more than a few . . ."

"Naturally," Joyce said, "we kept our main strength in reserve, unrevealed."

"The Shanga reported nothing of this sort."

"Would you expect them to?" Joyce let that sink in before she went on. "Nor will you find the cache if you search the oasis. They did not resist our assault with fire, so the guns cannot have been in this neighborhood. Most likely someone took them away at once into the Yagola lands, to be distributed later."

"We shall see about this." Another Ancient clipped off the words. "Guard!" A sentry came in through the doorway to the entry tunnel. "Fetch the spokesman of our clan guests."

Joyce brought Van Rijn up to date while they waited. "Goes well so far," the merchant said. "But next comes the ticklish part, not so much fun as tickling you."

"Really!" She drew herself up, hot in the face. "You're impossible."

"No, just improbable . . . Ah, here we go already."

A lean t'Kelan in Shanga garb trod into the room. He folded his arms and glowered at the Rokulela. "This is Batuzi's son Masotu," Akulo introduced. He leaned forward, tense as his colleagues. "The sky-folk have said you took many terrible weapons from their camp. Is that truth?"

Masotu started. "Certainly not! There was nothing but that one emptied handgun I showed you when you came down at dawn."

"So the Ancients were indeed in league with the Shanga," rasped a t'Kelan in Van Rijn's party.

Briefly disconcerted, Akulo collected himself and said in a steel tone, "Very well. Why should we deny it, after all? Kusulongo the City seeks the good of the whole world, which is its own good; and these sly strangers were bringing new ways that rotted old usage. Were they not softening you for the invasion of their own people? What other reason had they to travel about in your lands? What other reason could they have? Yes, this council urged the Shanga to wipe them out as they deserve."

Though her heartbeat nearly drowned her words, Joyce managed to interpret for Van Rijn. The merchant's lips thinned. "Now they confess it to our facing," he said. "Yet they have got to have some story ready to fob off Earthships and make humans never want to come here again. They do not intend to let us go down this hill alive, I see, and talk contradictions afterwards." But he gave her no word for the natives.

Akulo pointed at Masotu. "Do you tell us, then, that the sky-folk have lied and you found no arsenal?"

"Yes." The Shanga traded stares with Nyaronga. "Ah, your folk fretted lest we use that power to overrun your grasslands," he deduced shrewdly. "There was no need to fear. Go back in peace and let us finish dealing with the aliens."

"We never *feared*," Nyaronga corrected. Nonetheless his glance toward the humans was doubtful.

An Ancient stirred impatiently on the dais. "Enough of this," he said. "Now we have all seen still another case of the sky-fold brewing trouble. Call in the guards to slay them. Let peace be said between Shanga and all Rokulela. Send everyone home and have done."

Joyce finished her running translation as Akulo opened his mouth. "Botulism and bureaucrats!" Van Rijn exploded. "Not this fast, little chum." He reached under the recycler tank on his back and pulled out his blaster. "Please to keep still."

No t'Kelan stirred, though a hiss went among them. Van Rijn backed toward the wall so he could cover the doorway as well. "Now we talk more friendly," he smiled.

"The law has been broken," Akulo sputtered.

"Likewise the truce which you said between us," Joyce answered, though no culture on this planet regarded oath-breaking as anything but a peccadillo. She felt near fainting with relief. Not that the blaster solved many

problems. It wouldn't get them out of a city aswarm with
archers and spear-casters. But—

"Quiet!" boomed Van Rijn. Echoes rang from wall to
stony wall. A couple of sentries darted in. They pulled up
short when they saw the gun.

"Come on, join the party," the Earthman invited. "Lots
of room and energy charges for everybodies."

To Joyce he said, "Hokay, now is where we find out
whether we have brains enough to get out of being heroes.
Tell them that Nicholas Van Rijn has a speech to make,
then talk for me as I go along."

Weakly, she relayed the message. The least relaxation
showed on the tigery bodies before her. Akulo, Nyaronga,
and Masotu nodded together. "Let him be heard," the Ancient said. "There is always time to fight afterward."

"Good." Van Rijn's giant form took a step forward. He
swept the blaster muzzle around in an oratorical gesture.
"First, you should know I caused all this hullaballoo
mainly so we could talk. If I come back here alone, you
would have clobbered me with pointy little rocks, and that
would not be so good for any of us. Ergo, I had to come in
company. Let Nyaronga tell you I can fight like a hungry
creditor if needful. But maybe there is no need this time,
ha?"

Joyce passed on his words, sentence by sentence, and
waited while the Gangu pride-father confirmed that humans were tough customers. Van Rijn took advantage of
the general surprise to launch a quick verbal offensive.

"We have got this situation. Suppose the Shanga are lying and have really coppered a modern arsenal. Then
they can gain such power that even this city becomes a
client of theirs instead of being *primus inter pares* like before. *Nie?* To prevent this, a common cause is needful between Ancients, Rokulela, and us humans who can get
bigger weapons to stop the Yagola when our rescue ship
comes in."

"But we have no such booty," Masotu insisted.

"So you say," Joyce replied. She was beginning to get

Van Rijn's general idea. "Ancients and Rokulela, dare you take his word on so weighty a matter?"

As indecision waxed on the dais, Van Rijn continued. "Now let us on the other hands suppose I am the liar and there never was any loose zappers in the dome. Then Shanga and Ancients must keep on working together. For my people's ship that will come from our own territory, which is the whole skyful of stars, they must be told some yarn about why their dome was destroyed. Everybody but me and this cute doll here got safe away, so it will be known the Shanga did the job. Our folks will be angry at losing such a good chance for profit they have been working on for a long time. They will blame the Ancients as using Shanga for pussyfoots, and maybe blow this whole mountain to smitherlets, unless a good story that Shanga corroborate in every way has been cooked beforehand to clear the Ancients. Right? *Ja*. Well, then, for years to come, the Shanga—through them, all Yagola—must be in close touch with Kusulongo town. And they will not take the blame for no payment at all, will they? So hokay, you Rokulela, how impartial you think the Ancients will be to you? How impartial can the Ancients be, when the Shanga can blackmail them? You need humans here to make a balance."

Uulobu clashed his teeth together and cried, "This is true!" But Joyce watched Nyaronga. The chief pondered a long while, trading looks with his colleagues, before he said, "Yes, this may well be. At least, one does not wish to risk being cheated, when disputes come here for judgment. Also, the bad years may come to Yagolaland next, when they must move elsewhere . . . and a single failure to predict a flare for us could weaken our whole country for invasion."

Stillness stretched. Joyce's phone pickup sent her only the sputter of torches and the boom of wind beyond the doorway. Akulo stared down Van Rijn's gun muzzle, without a move. At last he said, "You sow discord with great skill, stranger. Do you think we can let so dangerous a one, or these pride-fathers whom you have now made into firm allies, leave here alive?"

"*Ja*," answered Van Rijn complacently through Joyce. "Because I did not really stir up trouble, only prove to your own big benefits that you can't trust each other and need human peoples to keep order. For see you, with humans and their weapons around, who have an interest in peace between clans and Hordes, some Yagola with a few guns can't accomplish anything. Or if they truly don't have guns, there is still no reason for the city to work foot in shoe with them if humans return peacefully and do not want revenge for their dome. So either way, the right balance is restored between herders and town. Q.E.D."

"But why should the sky-folk wish to establish themselves here?" Akulo argued. "Is your aim to take over the rightful functions of Kusulongo the City? No, first you must slay each one of us on the mountain!"

"Not needful," Van Rijn said. "We make our profit other ways. I have asked out the lady here about the facts while we was en route, and she dovetails very pretty, let me tell you. Uh . . . Joyce . . . you take over now. I am not sure how to best get the notion across when they haven't much chemical theory."

Her mouth fell open. "Do you mean—Nick, do you have an answer?"

"*Ja, ja, ja.*" He rubbed his hands and beamed. "I worked that out fine. Like follows: My own company takes over operations on t'Kela. You Esperancers help us get started, natural, but after that you can go spend your money on some other planet gone to seed . . . while Nicholas van Rijn takes money out of this one."

"What, what are you thinking?"

"Look, I want *kungu* wine, and a fur trade on the side might also be nice to have. The clans everywhere will bring me this stuff. I sell them ammonia and nitrates from the nitrogen-fixing plants we build, in exchange. They will need this to enrich their soils—also they will need to cultivate nitrogen-fixing bacteira the way you show them

—to increase crop yields so they can buy still more ammonia and nitrates. Of course, what they will really do this for is to get surplus credit for buying modern gadgets. Guns, especial. Nobody with hunter instincts can resist buying guns; he will even become a part-time farmer to do it. But also my factors will sell them tools and machines and stuff, what makes them slowly more civilized the way you want them to be. On all these deals, Solar Spice & Liquors turns a pretty good profit."

"But we didn't come to exploit them!"

Van Rijn chuckled. He reached up to twirl his mustache, clanked a hand against his helmet, made a face, and said, "Maybe you Esperancers didn't, but I sure did. And don't you see, this they can understand, the clans. Charity is outside their instincts, but profit is not, and they will feel good at how they swindle us on the price of wine. No more standoffishness and suspicion about humans—not when humans is plainly come here on a money hunt. You see?"

She nodded, half dazed. They weren't going to like this on Esperance; the Commonalty looked down from a lofty moral position on the Polesotechnic League; but they weren't fanatical about it, and if this was the only way the job could be one—Wait. "The Ancients," she objected. "How will you conciliate them? Introducing so many new elements is bound to destroy the basis of their whole economy."

"Oh, I already got that in mind. We will want plenty of native agents and clerks, smart fellows who keep records and expand our market territory and cetera. That takes care of many young Ancients . . . silly name. . . . As for the rest, though, maintaining the power and prestiges of the city as a unit, that we can also do. Remember, there are oil wells to develop and electrolysis plants to build. The electrolyzer plants will sell hydrogen to the ammonia plants, and the oil-burning operation can sell electricity. Hokay, so I build these oil and electrolyzer plants, turn them over to the Ancients to run, and let the Ancients buy them from me on a long-term mortgage. So profitable and key facilities should suit them very well, *nie?*" He stared thoughtfully into a dark corner. "Um-m-m . . . do you think I can get twenty percent interest, compounded annual, or must I have to settle for fifteen?"

Joyce gasped a while before she could start searching for Kusulongo phrases.

They went down the mountain toward sunset, with cheers at their back and campfires twinkling below to welcome them. Somehow the view seemed brighter to Joyce than ever erenow. And there was beauty in that illimitable westward plain, where a free folk wandered through their own lives. The next few weeks, waiting for the ship, won't be bad at all, she thought. In fact, they should be fun.

"Another advantage," Van Rijn told her smugly, "is that making a commercial operation with profit for everybody out of this is a much better guarantee the job will be continued for long enough to save the planet. You thought your government could do it. Bah! Governments is dayflies. Any change of ideology, of mood, even, and poof goes your project. But private action, where everybody concerned is needful to everybody else's income, that's stable. Politics, they come and go, but greed goes on forever."

"Oh, no, that can't be," she denied.

"Well, we got time in the car to argue about it, and about much else." Van Rijn said. "I think I can rig a little still to get the alcohol out of *kungu*. Then we put it in fruit juice and have a sort of wine with our meals like human beings, by damn!"

"I . . . I shouldn't, Nicky . . . that is, well, us two alone—"

"You is only young once. You mean a poor old man like me has got to show you how to be young?" Van Rijn barely suppressed a leer. "Hokay, fine by me."

Joyce looked away, flushing. She'd have to maintain a strict watch on him till the ship arrived, she thought. And on herself, for that matter.

Of course, if she did happen to relax just the littlest bit . . . after all, he really was a very interesting person . . .

A loftier Argo cleaves the main,
Fraught with a later prize;
Another Orpheus sings again,
And loves, and weeps, and dies.
A new Ulysses leaves once more
Calypso for his native shore.

              —Shelley

THE MASTER KEY

Once upon a time there was a king who set himself above the foreign merchants. What he did is of no account now; it was long ago and on another planet, and besides, the wench is dead. Harry Stenvik and I hung him by the seat of his trousers from his tallest minaret, in sight of all the people, and the name of the Polesotechnic League was great in the land. Then we made inroads on the stock-in-trade of the Solar Spice & Liquors Company factor and swore undying brotherhood.

Now there are those who maintain that Nicholas van Rijn has a cryogenic computer in that space used by the ordinary Terran for storing his heart. This may be so. But he does not forget a good workman. And I know no reason why he should have invited me to dinner except that Harry would be there, and—this being the briefest of business trips to Earth for me—we would probably have no other chance of meeting.

The flitter set me off atop the Winged Cross, where Van Rijn keeps what he honestly believes is a modest little penthouse apartment. A summer's dusk softened the mass of lesser buildings that stretched to the horizon and beyond; Venus had wakened in the west and Chicago Integrate was opening multitudinous lights. This high up, only a low machine throb reached my ears. I walked among roses and jasmine to the door. When it scanned me and dilated, Harry was waiting. We fell into each other's arms

116

and praised God with many loud violations of His third commandment.

Afterward we stood apart and looked. "You haven't changed much," he lied. "Mean and ugly as ever. Methane in the air must agree with you."

"Ammonia, where I've been of late," I corrected him. "S.O.P.: occassional bullets and endless dickering. *You're* disgustingly sleek and contented. How's Sigrid?" As it must to all men, domesticity had come to him. In his case it lasted, and he had built a house on the cliffs above Hardanger Fjord and raised mastiffs and sons. Myself—but that also is irrelevant.

"Fine. She sends her love and a box of her own cookies. Next time you must wangle a longer stay and come see us."

"The boys?"

"Same." The soft Norse accent roughened the least bit. "Per's had his troubles, but they are mending. He's here tonight."

"Well, great." The last I'd heard of Harry's oldest son, he was an apprentice aboard one of Van Rijn's ships, somewhere in the Hercules region. But that was several years ago, and you can rise fast in the League if you survive. "I imagine he has master's rank by now."

"Yes, quite newly. Plus an artificial femur and a story to tell. Come, let's join them."

Hm, I thought, so Old Nick was economizing on his bird-killing stones again. He had enough anecdotes of his own that he didn't need to collect them, unless they had some special use to him. A gesture of kindness might as well be thrown into the interview.

We passed through the foyer and crossed a few light-years of trollcat rug to the far end of the living room. Three men sat by the viewer wall, at the moment transparent to sky and city. Only one of them rose. He had been seated a little to one side, in a tigery kind of relaxed alertness—a stranger to me, dark and lean, with a blaster that had seen considerable service at his hip.

Nicholas van Rijn wallowed his bulk deeper into his lounger, hoisted a beer stein and roared, "Ha! Welcome to you, Captain, and you will maybe have a small drink like me before dinner?" After which he tugged his goatee and muttered, "Gabriel will tootle before I get you bepestered Anglic through this poor old noggin. I think I have just called myself a small drink."

I bowed to him as is fitting to a merchant prince, turned, and gave Per Stenvik my hand. "Excuse my staying put," he said. His face was still pale and gaunt; health was coming back, but youth never would. "I got a trifle clobbered."

"So I heard," I answered. "Don't worry, it'll heal up. I hate to think how much of me is replacement by now, but as long as the important parts are left . . ."

"Oh, yes, I'll be okay. Thanks to Manuel. Uh, Manuel Felipe Gomez y Palomares of Nuevo México. My ensign."

I introduced myself with great formality, according to what I knew of customs of those poor and haughty colonists from the far side of Arcturus. His courtesy was equal, before he turned to make sure the blanket was secure around Per's legs. Nor did he go back to his seat and his glass of claret before Harry and I lowered ourselves. A human servant—male, in this one Van Rijn establishment —brought us our orders, *akvavit* for Harry and a martini for me. Per fiddled with a glass of Ansan vermouth.

"How long will you be home?" I asked him after the small talk had gone by.

"As long as needful," Harry said quickly.

"No more, though," Van Rijn said with equal speed. "Not one millimoment more can he loaf than nature must have; and he is young and strong."

"Pardon, *señor*," Manuel said—how softly and deferentially, and with what a clang of colliding stares. "I would not gainsay my superiors. But my duty is to know how it is with my captain, and the doctors are fools. He shall rest not less than till the Day of the Dead; and then surely, with the Nativity so near, the *señor* will not deny him the holidays at home?"

Van Rijn threw up his hands. "Everyone, they call me apocalyptic beast," he wailed, "and I am only a poor lonely old man in a sea of grievances, trying so hard to keep awash. One good boy with promises I find, I watch him from before his pants dry out for I know his breed. I give him costly schooling in hopes he does not turn out another curdlebrain, and no sooner does he not but he is in the locker and my fine new planet gets thrown to the wolves!"

"Lord help the wolves," Per grinned. "Don't worry, sir, I'm as anxious to get back as you are."

"Hoy, hoy, I am not going. I am too old and fat. Ah, you think you have troubles now, but wait till time has gnawed you down to a poor old wheezer like me who has not even any pleasures left. Abdul! Abdul, you jellylegs, bring drink, you want we should dry up and puff away? . . . What, only me ready for a refill?"

"Do you really want to see that Helheim again?" Harry asked, with a stiff glance at Van Rijn.

"Judas, yes," Per said. "It's just waiting for the right man. A whole *world,* Dad! Don't you remember?"

Harry looked through the wall and nodded. I made haste to intrude on his silence. "What were you there after, Per?"

"Everything," the young man said. "I told you it's an entire planet. Not one percent of the land surface has been mapped."

"Huh? Not even from orbit?"

Manuel's expression showed me what they thought of orbital maps.

"But for a starter, what attracted us in the first place, furs and herbs," Per said. Wordlessly, Manuel took a little box from his pocket, opened it, and handed it to me. A bluish-green powder of leaves lay within. I tasted. There was a sweet-sour flavor with wild overtones, and the odor went to the oldest, deepest part of my brain and roused memories I had not known were lost.

"The chemicals we have not yet understood and synthesized," Van Rijn rumbled around the cigar he was lighting. "Bah! What do my chemists do all day but play happy fun games in the lab alcohol? And the furs, *ja,* I have Lupescu of the Peltery volcanomaking that he must buy them from me. He is even stooping to spies, him, he has the ethics of a paranoid weasel. Fifteen thousand he spent last month alone, trying to find where that planet is."

"How do you know how much he spent?" Harry asked blandly.

Van Rijn managed to look smug and hurt at the same time.

Per said with care, "I'd better not mention the coordinates myself. It's out Pegasus way. A G-nine dwarf star, about half as luminous as Sol. Eight planets, one of them terrestroid. Brander came upon it in the course of a survey, thought it looked interesting, and settled down to learn more. He'd really only time to tape the language of the locality where he was camped, and do the basic-basic planetography and bionics. But he did find out about the furs and herbs. So I was sent to establish a trading post."

"His first command," Harry said, unnecessarily on any-one's account but his own.

"Trouble with the natives, eh?" I asked.

"Trouble is not the word," Van Rijn said. "The word is not for polite ears." He dove into his beer stein and came up snorting. "After all I have done for them, the saints keep on booting me in the soul like this."

"But we seem to have it licked," Per said.

"Ah. You think so?" Van Rijn waggled a hairy fore-finger at him. "That is what we should like to be more sure of, boy, before we send out and maybe lose some expensive ships."

"*Y algunos hombres buenos,*" Manuel muttered, so low he could scarcely be heard. One hand dropped to the butt of his gun.

"I have been reading the reports from Brander's people," Van Rijn said. "Also your own. I think maybe I see a pattern. When you have been swindling on so many planets like me, new captain, you will have analogues at your digits for much that is new. . . . Ah, pox and pity it is to get jaded!" He puffed a smoke ring that settled around Per's bright locks. "Still, you are never sure. I think sometimes God likes a little practical joke on us poor mortals, when we get too cockish. So I jump on no conclusions before I have heard from your own teeth how it was. Reports, even on visitape, they have no more flavor than what my competition sells. In you I live again the fighting and merrylarks, everything that is now so far behind me in my doting."

This from the single-handed conqueror of Borthu, Diomedes, and t'Kela!

"Well—" Per blushed and fumbled with his glass. "There really isn't a lot to tell, you know. I mean, each of you freemen has been through so much more than—uh—one silly episode . . ."

Harry gestured at the blanketed legs. "Nothing silly there," he said.

Per's lips tightened. "I'm sorry. You're right. Men died."

Chiefly because it is not good to dwell overly long on those lost from a command of one's own, I said, "What's the planet like? 'Terrestroid' is a joke. They sit in an Earthside office and call it that if you can breathe the air."

"And not fall flat in an oof from the gravity for at least half an hour, and not hope the *whole* year round you have no brass-monkey ancestors." Van Rijn's nod sent the black ringlets swirling around his shoulder.

"I generally got assigned to places where the brass monkeys melted," Harry complained.

"Well, Cain isn't too bad in the low latitudes," Per said. His face relaxed, and his hands came alive in quick gestures that reminded me of his mother. "It's about Earth-size, average orbital radius a little over one A.U. Denser atmosphere, though, by around fifteen percent, which makes for more greenhouse effect. Twenty-hour rotation period; no moons. Thirty-two degrees of axial tilt, which does rather complicate the seasons. But we were at fifteen-forty north, in fairly low hills, and it was summer. A nearby pool was frozen every morning, and snowbanks remained on the slopes—but really, not bad for the planet of a G-nine star."

"Did Brander name it Cain?" I asked.

"Yes. I don't know why. But it turned out appropriate. Too damned appropriate." Again the bleakness. Manuel took his captain's empty glass and glided off, to return in a moment with it filled. Per drank hurriedly.

"Always there is trouble," Van Rijn said. "You will learn."

"But the mission was going so well!" Per protested. "Even the language and the data seemed to . . . to flow into my head on the voyage out. In fact, the whole crew learned easily." He turned to me. "There were twenty of us on the *Miriam Knight*. She's a real beauty, Cheland-class transport, built for speed rather than capacity, you know. More wasn't needed, when we were only supposed to erect the first post and get the idea of regular trade across to the autochthones. We had the usual line of goods, fabrics, tools, weapons, household stuff like scissors and meat grinders. Not much ornament, because Brander's xenologists hadn't been able to work out any consistent pattern for it. Individual Cainites seemed to dress and decorate themselves any way they pleased. In the Ulash area, at least, which of course was the only one we had any details on."

"And damn few there," Harry murmured. "Also as usual."

"Agriculture?" I inquired.

"Some primitive cultivation," Per said. "Small plots scratched out of the forest, tended by the Lugals. In Ulash a little metallurgy has begun, copper, gold, silver, but even they are essentially neolithic. And essentially hunters —the Yildivans, that is—along with such Lugals as they employ to help. The food supply is mainly game. In fact, the better part of what farming is done is to supply fabric."

"What do they look like, these people?"

"I've a picture here." Per reached in his tunic and handed me a photograph. "That's old Shivaru. Early in our acquaintance. He was probably scared of the camera but damned if he'd admit it. You'll notice the Lugal he has with him is frankly in a blue funk."

I studied the image with an interest that grew. The background was harsh plutonic hillside, where grass of a pale yellowish turquoise grew between dark boulders. But on the right I glimpsed a densely wooded valley. The sky overhead was wan, and the orange sunlight distorted colors.

Shivaru stood very straight and stiff, glaring into the lens. He was about two meters tall, Per said, his body build much like that of a long-legged, deep-chested man. Tawny, spotted fur covered him to the end of an elegant tail. The head was less anthropoid: a black ruff on top, slit-pupiled green eyes, round mobile ears, flat nose that looked feline even to the cilia around it, full-lipped mouth with protruding tushes at the corners, and jaw that tapered down to a V. He wore a sort of loincloth, gaudily dyed, and a necklace of raw semiprecious stones. His left hand clutched an obsidian-bladed battle-ax and there was a steel trade-knife in his belt.

"They're mammals, more or less," Per said, "though with any number of differences in anatomy and chemistry, as you'd expect. They don't sweat, however. There's a complicated system of exo- and endothermic reactions in the blood to regulate temperature."

"Sweating is not so common on cold terrestroids," Van Rijn remarked. "Always you find analogs to something you met before, if you look long enough. Evolution makes parallels."

"And skew lines," I added. "Uh—Brander got some corpses to dissect, then?"

"Well, not any Yildivans," Per said. "But they sold him as many dead Lugals as he asked for, who're obviously of the same genus." He winced. "I hope to hell they didn't kill the Lugals especially for that purpose."

My attention had gone to the creature that cowered behind Shivaru. It was a squat, short-shanked, brown-furred version of the other Cainite. Forehead and chin were poorly developed and the muzzle had not yet become a nose. The being was nude except for a heavy pack, a quiver of arrows, a bow, and two spears piled on its muscular back. I could see that the skin was rubbed naked and calloused by such burdens. "This is a Lugal?" I pointed.

"Yes. You see, there are two related species on the planet, one farther along in evolution than the other. As if Australopithecus had survived till today on Earth. The Yildivans have made slaves of the Lugals—certainly in Ulash, and as far as we could find out by spot checks, everywhere on Cain."

"Pretty roughly treated, aren't they, the poor devils?" Harry said. "*I* wouldn't trust a slave with weapons."

"But Lugals are completely trustworthy," Per said. "Like dogs. They do the hard, monotonous work. The Yildivans—male and female—are the hunters, artists, magicians, everything that matters. That is, what culture exists is Yildivan." He scowled into his drink. "Though I'm not sure how meaningful 'culture' is in this connection."

"How so?" Van Rijn lifted brows far above his small black eyes.

"Well . . . they, the Yildivans, haven't anything like a nation, a tribe, any sort of community. Family groups split up when the cubs are old enough to fend for themselves. A young male establishes himself somewhere, chases off all comers, and eventually one or more young females come join him. Their Lugals tag along, naturally —like dogs again. As near as I could learn, such families have only the most casual contact. Occasional barter, occasional temporary gangs formed to hunt extra-large animals, occasional clashes between individuals, and that's about it."

"But hold on," I objected. "Intelligent races need more. Something to be the carrier of tradition, something to stimulate the evolution of brain, a way for individuals to communicate ideas to each other. Else intelligence hasn't got any biological function."

"I fretted over that too," Per said. "Had long talks with Shivaru, Fereghir, and others who drifted into camp whenever they felt like it. We really tried hard to understand each other. They were as curious about us as we about them, and as quick to see the mutual advantage in trade relations. But what a job! A whole different planet—two or three billion years of separate evolution—and we had only pidgin Ulash to start with, the limited vocabulary Brander's people had gotten. We couldn't go far into the subtleties. Especially when they, of course, took everything about their own way of life for granted.

"Toward the end, though, I began to get a glimmering. It turns out that in spite of their oafish appearance, the Lugals are not stupid. Maybe even as bright as their masters, in a different fashion; at any rate, not too far behind them. And—in each of these family groups, these patriarchal settlements in a cave or hut, way off in the forest, there are several times as many Lugals as Yildivans. Every member of the family, even the kids, has a number of slaves. Thus you may not get Yildivan clans or tribes, but you do get the numerical equivalent among the Lugals.

"Then the Lugals are sent on errands to other Yildivan preserves, with messages or barter goods or whatever, and bring back news. And they get traded around; the Yildivans breed them deliberately, with a shrewd practical grasp of genetics. Apparently, too, the Lugals are often allowed to wander off by themselves when there's no work for them to do—much as we let our dogs run loose—and hold powwows of their own.

"You mustn't think of them as being mistreated. They

are, by our standards, but Cain is a brutal place and Yildivans don't exactly have an easy life either. An intelligent
Lugal is valued. He's made straw boss over the others,
teaches the Yildivan young special skills and songs and
such, is sometimes even asked by his owner what he
thinks ought to be done in a given situation. Some families
let him eat and sleep in their own dwelling, I'm told. And
remember, his loyalty is strictly to the masters. What
they may do to other Lugals is nothing to him. He'll
gladly help cull the weaklings, punish the lazy, anything.

"So, to get to the point, I think that's your answer. The
Yildivans do have a community life, a larger society—but
indirectly, through their Lugals. The Yildivans are the
creators and innovators, the Lugals the communicators
and preservers. I daresay the relationship has existed for
so long a time that the biological evolution of both species
has been conditioned by it."

"You speak rather well of them," said Harry grimly,
"considering what they did to you."

"But they were very decent people at first." I could
hear in Per's voice how hurt he was by that which had
happened. "Proud as Satan, callous, but not cruel. Honest
and generous. They brought gifts whenever they arrived,
with no thought of payment. Two or three offered to assign
us Lugal laborers. That wasn't necessary or feasible when
we had machinery along, but they didn't realize it then.
When they did, they were quick to grasp the idea, and
mightily impressed. I think. Hard to tell, because they
couldn't or wouldn't admit anyone else might be superior
to them. That is, each individual thought of himself as
being as good as anyone else anywhere in the world. But
they seemed to regard us as their equals. I didn't try to
explain where we were really from. 'Another country'
looked sufficient for practical purposes.

"Shivaru was especially interested in us. He was mid-
dle-aged, most of his children grown and moved away.
Wealthy in local terms, progressive—he was experimenting
with ranching as a supplement to hunting—and his advice

was much sought after by the others. I took him for a ride in a flitter and he was happy and excited as any child; brought his three mates along next time so they could enjoy it too. We went hunting together occasionally. Lord, you should have seen him run down those great horned beasts, leap on their backs, and brain them with one blow of that tremendous ax! Then his Lugals would butcher the game and carry it home to camp. The meat tasted damn good, believe me. Cainite biochemistry lacks some of our vitamins, but otherwise a human can get along all right there.

"Mainly, though, I remember how we'd talk. I suppose it's old hat to you freemen, but I had never before spent hour after hour with another being, both of us at work trying to build up a vocabulary and an understanding, both getting such a charge out of it that we'd forget even to eat until Manuel or Cherkez—that was his chief Lugal, a gnarly, droll old fellow, made me think of the friendly gnomes in my fairy tale books when I was a youngster—until one of them would tell us. Sometimes my mind wandered off and I'd come back to earth realizing that I'd just sat there admiring his beauty. Yildivans are as graceful as cats, as pleasing in shape as a good gun. And as deadly, when they want to be. I found that out!

"We had a favorite spot, in the lee of a cottage-sized boulder on the hillside above camp. The rock was warm against our backs; seemed even more so when I looked at that pale shrunken sun and my breath smoking out white across the purplish sky. Far, far overhead a bird of prey would wheel, then suddenly stoop—in the thick air I could hear the whistle through its wing feathers—and vanish into the treetops down in the valley. Those leaves had a million different shades of color, like an endless autumn.

"Shivaru squatted with his tail curled around his knees, ax on the ground beside him. Cherkez and one or two other Lugals hunkered at a respectful distance. Their eyes never left their Yildivan. Sometimes Manuel joined us, when he wasn't busy bossing some phase of construction.

Remember, Manuel? You really shouldn't have kept so quiet."

"Silence was fitting, Captain," said the Nuevo Méxican.

"Well," Per said, "Shivaru's deep voice would go on and on. He was full of plans for the future. No question of a trade treaty—no organization for us to make a treaty with —but he foresaw his people bringing us what we wanted in exchange for what we offered. And he was bright enough to see how the existence of a central mart like this, a common meeting ground, would affect them. More joint undertakings would be started. The idea of close cooperation would take root. He looked forward to that, within the rather narrow limits he could conceive. For instance, many Yildivans working together could take real advantage of the annual spawning run up the Mukushyat River. Big canoes could venture across a strait he knew of, to open fresh hunting grounds. That sort of thing.

"But then in a watchtick his ears would perk, his whiskers vibrate, he'd lean forward and start to ask about my own people. What sort of country did we come from? How was the game there? What were our mating and childrearing practices? How did we ever produce such beautiful things? Oh, he had the whole cosmos to explore! Bit by bit, as my vocabulary grew, his questions got less practical and more abstract. So did mine, naturally. We were getting at each other's psychological foundations now, and were equally fascinated.

"I was not too surprised to learn that his culture had no religion. In fact, he was hard put to understand my questions about it. They practiced magic, but looked on it simply as a kind of technology. There was no animism, no equivalent of anthropomorphism. A Yildivan knew too damn well he was superior to any plant or animal. I think, but I'm not sure, that they had some vague concept of reincarnation. But it didn't interest them much, apparently, and the problem of origins hadn't occurred. Life was what you had, here and now. The world was a set of phenomena, to live with or master or be defeated by as the case might be.

"Shivaru asked me why I'd asked him about such a self-evident thing."

Per shook his head. His glance went down to the blanket around his lap and quickly back again. "That may have been my first mistake."

"No, Captain," said Manuel most gently. "How could you know they lacked souls?"

"Do they?" Per mumbled.

"We leave that to the theologians," Van Rijn said. "They get paid to decide. Go on, boy."

I could see Per brace himself. "I tried to explain the idea of God," he said tonelessly. "I'm pretty sure I failed. Shivaru acted puzzled and . . . troubled. He left soon after. The Yildivans of Ulash use drums for long-range communication, have I mentioned? All that night I heard the drums mutter in the valley and echo from the cliffs. We had no visitors for a week. But Manuel, scouting around in the area, said he'd found tracks and traces. We were being watched.

"I was relieved, at first, when Shivaru returned. He had a couple of others with him, Fereghir and Tulitur, important males like himself. They came straight across the hill toward me. I was supervising the final touches on our timber-cutting system. We were to use local lumber for most of our construction, you see. Cut and trim in the woods with power beams, load the logs on a gravsled for the sawmill, then snake them directly through the induration vats to the site, where the foundations had now been laid. The air was full of whine and crash, boom and chug, in a wind that cut like a laser. I could hardly see our ship or our sealtents through dust, tinged bloody in the sun.

"They came to me, those three tall hunters, with a dozen armed Lugals hovering behind. Shivaru beckoned. 'Come,' he said. 'This is no place for a Yildivan.' I looked him in the eyes and they were filmed over, as if he'd put a glass mask between me and himself. Frankly, my skin prickled. I was unarmed—everybody was except Manuel, you know what Nuevo Méxicans are—and I was afraid I'd precipitate something by going for a weapon. In fact, I even made a point of speaking Ulash as I ordered Tom Bullis to take over for me and told Manuel to come along uphill. If the autochthones had taken some notion into their heads that we were planning harm, it wouldn't do for them to hear us use a language they didn't know.

"Not another word was spoken till we were out of the dust and racket, at the old place by the boulder. It didn't feel warm today. Nothing did. 'I welcome you,' I said to the Yildivans, 'and bid you dine and sleep with us.' That's the polite formula when a visitor arrives. I didn't get the regular answer.

"Tulitur hefted the spear he carried and asked—not rudely, understand, but with a kind of shiver in the tone —'Why have you come to Ulash?'

" 'Why?' I stuttered. 'You know. To trade.'

" 'No, wait, Tulitur,' Shivaru interrupted. 'Your question is blind.' He turned to me. 'Were you sent?' he asked. And what I would like to ask you sometime, freemen, is whether it makes sense to call a voice black.

"I couldn't think of any way to hedge. Something had gone awry, but I'd no feeblest notion what. A lie or a stall was as likely, *a priori,* to make matters worse as the truth. I saw the sunlight glisten along that dark ax head and felt most infernally glad to have Manuel beside me. Even so, the noise from the camp sounded faint and distant. Or was it only that the wind was whittering louder?

"I made myself stare back at him. 'You know we are here on behalf of others like us at home,' I said. The muscles tightened still more under his fur. Also . . . I can't read nonhuman expressions especially well. But Fereghir's lips were drawn off his teeth as if he confronted an enemy. Tulitur had grounded his spear, point down. Brander's reports observed that a Yildivan never did that in the presence of a friend. Shivaru, though, was hardest to understand. I could have sworn he was grieved.

" 'Did God send you?' he asked.

"That put the dunce's cap on the whole lunatic business. I actually laughed, though I didn't feel at all funny. Inside my head it went click-click-click. I recognized a semantic point. Ulash draws some fine distinctions between various kinds of imperative. A father's command to his small child is entirely different—in word and concept both —from a command to another Yildivan beaten in a fight, which is different in turn from a command to a Lugal, and so on through a wider range than our psycholinguists have yet measured.

"Shivaru wanted to know if I was God's slave.

"Well, this was no time to explain the history of religion, which I'm none too clear about anyway. I just said no, I wasn't; God was a being in Whose existence some of us believed, but not everyone, and He had certainly not issued me any direct orders.

"That rocked them back! The breath hissed between Shivaru's fangs, his ruff bristled aloft and his tail whipped his legs. 'Then who did send you?' he nearly screamed. I could translate as well by: 'So who *is* your owner?'

"I heard a slither alongside me as Manuel loosened his gun in the holster. Behind the three Yildivans, the Lugals gripped their own axes and spears at the ready. You can imagine how carefully I picked my words. 'We are here freely,' I said, 'as part of an association.' Or maybe the word I had to use means 'fellowship'—I wasn't about to explain economics either. 'In our home country,' I said, 'none of us is a Lugal. You have seen our devices that work for us. We have no need of Lugalhood.'

" 'Ah-h-h,' Fereghir sighed, and poised his spear. Manuel's gun clanked free. 'I think best you go,' he said to them, 'before there is a fight. We do not wish to kill.'

"Brander had made a point of demonstrating guns, and so had we. No one stirred for a time that went on eternally, in that Fimbul wind. The hair stood straight on the Lugals.

They were ready to rush us and die at a word. But it wasn't forthcoming. Finally the three Yildivans exchanged glances. Shivaru said in a dead voice, 'Let us consider this thing.' They turned on their heels and walked off through the long, whispering grass, their pack close around them.

"The drums beat for days and nights.

"We considered the thing ourselves at great length. What was the matter, anyhow? The Yildivans were primitive and unsophisticated by Commonwealth standards, but not stupid. Shivaru had not been surprised at the ways we differed from his people. For instance, the fact that we lived in communities instead of isolated families had only been one more oddity about us, intriguing rather than shocking. And, as I've told you, while large-scale cooperation among Yildivans wasn't common, it did happen once in a while; so what was wrong with our doing likewise?

"Igor Yuschenkoff, the captain of the *Miriam,* had a reasonable suggestion. 'If they have gotten the idea that we are slaves,' he said, 'then our masters must be still more powerful. Can they think we are preparing a base for invasion?'

" 'But I told them plainly we are not slaves,' I said.

" 'No doubt.' He laid a finger alongside his nose. 'Do they believe you?'

"You can imagine how I tossed awake in my sealtent. Should we haul gravs altogether, find a different area and start afresh? That would mean scrapping nearly everything we'd done. A whole new language to learn was the least of the problems. Nor would a move necessarily help. Scouting trips by flitter had indicated pretty strongly that the same basic pattern of life prevailed everywhere on Cain, as it did on Earth in the paleolithic era. If we'd run afoul, not of some local taboo, but of some fundamental . . . I just didn't know. I doubt if Manuel spent more then two hours a night in bed. He was too busy tightening our system of guards, drilling the men, prowling around to inspect and keep them alert.

"But our next contact was peaceful enough on the surface. One dawn a sentry roused me to say that a bunch of natives were here. Fog had arisen overnight, turned the world into wet gray smoke where you couldn't see three meters. As I came outside I heard the drip off a trac parked close by, the only clear sound in the muffledness. Tulitur and another Yildivan stood at the edge of camp, with about fifty male Lugals behind. Their fur sheened with water, and their weapons were rime-coated. 'They must have traveled by night, Captain,' Manuel said, 'for the sake of cover. Surely others wait beyond view.' He led a squad with me.

"I made the Yildivans welcome, ritually, as if nothing had happened. I didn't get any ritual back. Tulitur said only, 'We are here to trade. For your goods we will return those furs and plants you desire.'

"That was rather jumping the gun, with our post still less than half built. But I couldn't refuse what might be an olive branch. 'That is well,' I said. 'Come, let us eat while we talk about it.' Clever move, I thought. Accepting someone's food puts you under the same sort of obligation in Ulash that it used to on Earth.

"Tulitur and his companion—Bokzahan, I remember the name now—didn't offer thanks, but they did come into the ship and sit at the mess table. I figured this would be more ceremonious and impressive than a tent; also, it was out of that damned raw cold. I ordered stuff like bacon and eggs that the Cainites were known to like. They got right to business. 'How much will you trade to us?'

" 'That depends on what you want, and on what you have to give in exchange,' I said, to match their curtness.

" 'We have brought nothing with us,' Bokzahan said, 'for we knew not if you would be willing to bargain.'

" 'Why should I not be?' I answered. 'That is what I came for. There is no strife between us.' And I shot at him: 'Is there?'

"None of those ice-green eyes wavered. 'No,' Tulitur said, 'there is not. Accordingly, we wish to buy guns.'

" 'Such things we may not sell,' I answered. Best not to add that policy allowed us to as soon as we felt reasonably sure no harm would result. 'However, we have knives to exchange, as well as many useful tools.'

"They sulked a bit, but didn't argue. Instead, they went right to work, haggling over terms. They wanted as much of everything as we'd part with, and really didn't try to bargain the price down far. Only they wanted the stuff on credit. They needed it now, they said, and it'd take time to gather the goods for payment.

"That put me in an obvious pickle. On the one hand, the Yildivans had always acted honorably and, as far as I could check, always spoken truth. Nor did I want to antagonize them. On the other hand—but you can fill that in for yourself. I flatter myself I gave them a diplomatic answer. We did not for an instant doubt their good intentions, I said. We knew the Yildivans were fine chaps. But accidents could happen, and if so, we'd be out of pocket by a galactic sum.

"Tulitur slapped the table and snorted, 'Such fears might have been expected. Very well, we shall leave our Lugals here until payment is complete. Their value is great. But then you must carry the goods where we want them.'

"I decided that on those terms they could have half the agreed amount right away."

Per fell silent and gnawed his lip. Harry leaned over to pat his hand. Van Rijn growled, "*Ja,* by damn, no one can foretell everything that goes wrong, only be sure that some bloody-be-plastered thing will. You did hokay, boy. . . . Abdul, more drink, you suppose maybe this is Mars?"

Per sighed. "We loaded the stuff on a gravsled," he went on. "Manuel accompanied in an armed flitter, as a precaution. But nothing happened. Fifty kilometers or so from camp, the Yildivans told our men to land near a river. They had canoes drawn onto the bank there, with a few other Yildivans standing by. Clearly they intended to float the goods further by themselves, and Manuel called me to see if I had any objections. 'No,' I said. 'What difference does it make? They must want to keep the destination secret. They don't trust us any longer.' Behind him, in the screen, I saw Bokzahan watching. Our communicators had fascinated visitors before now. But this time, was there some equivalent of a sneer on his face?

"I was busy arranging quarters and rations for the Lugals, though. And a guard or two, nothing obtrusive. Not that I really expected trouble. I'd heard their masters say, 'Remain here and do as the *Erziran* direct until we come for you.' But nevertheless it felt queasy, having that pack of dog-beings in camp.

"They settled down in their animal fashion. When the drums began again that night they got restless, shifted around in the pavilion we'd turned over to them and mewled in a language Brander hadn't recorded. But they were quite meek next morning. One of them even asked if they couldn't help in our work. I had to laugh at the thought of a Lugal behind the controls of a five hundred kilowatt trac, and told him no, thanks, they need only loaf and watch us. They were good at loafing.

"A few times, in the next three days, I tried to get them into conversation. But nothing came of that. They'd answer me, not in the deferential style they used to a Yildivan but not insolently either. However, the answers were meaningless. 'Where do you live?' I would say. 'In the forest yonder,' the slave replied, staring at his toes. 'What sort of tasks do you have to do at home?' 'That which my Yildivan sets for me.' I gave up.

"Yet they weren't stupid. They had some sort of game they played, involving figures drawn in the dirt, that I never did unravel. Each sundown they formed ranks and crooned, an eerie minor-key chant, with improvisations that sometimes sent a chill along my nerves. Mostly they slept, or sat and stared at nothing, but once in a while several would squat in a circle, arms around their neighbors' shoulders, and whisper together.

"Well . . . I'm making the story too long. We were attacked shortly before dawn of the fourth day.

"Afterward I learned that something like a hundred male Yildivans were in that party, and heaven knows how many Lugals. They'd rendezvoused from everywhere in that tremendous territory called Ulash, called by the drums and, probably, by messengers who'd run day and night through the woods. Our pickets were known to their scouts, and they laid a hurricane of arrows over those spots, while the bulk of them rushed in between. Otherwise I can't tell you much. I was a casualty." Per grimaced. "What a damn fool thing to happen. On my first command!"

"Go on," Harry urged. "You haven't told me any details."

"There aren't many," Per shrugged. "The first screams and roars slammed me awake. I threw on a jacket and stuffed feet into boots while my free hand buckled on a gun belt. By then the sirens were in full cry. Even so, I heard a blaster beam sizzle past my tent.

"I stumbled out into the compound. Everything was one black, boiling hell-kettle. Blasters flashed and flashed, sirens howled and voices cried battle. The cold stabbed at me. Starlight sheened on snowbanks and hoarfrost over the hills. I had an instant to think how bright and many the stars were, out there and not giving a curse.

"Then Yuschenkoff switched on the floodlamps in the *Miriam's* turret. Suddenly an aritficial sun stood overhead, too bright for us to look at. What must it have been to the Cainites? Blue-white incandescence, I suppose. They swarmed among our tents and machines, tall leopard-furred hunters, squat brown gnomes, axes, clubs, spears, bows, slings, our own daggers in their hands. I saw only one man—sprawled on the earth, gun still between his fingers, head a broken horror.

"I put the command mike to my mouth—always wore it on my wrist as per doctrine—and bawled out orders as I pelted toward the ship. We had the atom itself to fight for us, but we were twenty, no, nineteen or less, against Ulash.

"Now our dispositions were planned for defense. Two men slept in the ship, the others in sealtents ringed around her. The half dozen on guard duty had been cut off, but the rest had the ship for an impregnable retreat. What we must do, though, was rally to the rescue of those guards, and quick. If it wasn't too late.

"I saw the boys emerge from their strong point under the landing jacks. Even now I remember how Zerkowsky hadn't fastened his parka, and what a low-comedy way it flapped around his bottom. He didn't use pajamas. You notice the damnedest small things at such times, don't you? The Cainites had begun to mill about, dazzled by the light. They hadn't expected that, or the siren, which is a terrifying thing to hear at close range. Quite a few of them were already strewn dead or dying.

"Then—but all I knew personally was a tide that bellowed and yelped and clawed. It rolled over me from behind. I went down under their legs. They pounded across me and left me in the grip of a Lugal. He lay on my chest and went for my throat with teeth and hands. Judas, but that creature was strong! Centimeter by centimeter he closed in against my pushing and gouging. Suddenly another one got into the act. Must have snatched a club from some fallen Cainite and attacked whatever part of me was handiest, which happened to be my left shin. It's nothing but pain and rage after that, till the blessed darkness came.

"The fact was, of course, that our Lugal hostages had overrun their guards and broken free. I might have expected as much. Even without specific orders, they wouldn't have stood idle while their masters fought. But doubtless they'd been given advance commands. Tulitur and Bokzahan diddled us very nicely. First they got a big consignment of our trade goods, free, and then they planted reinforcements for themselves right in our compound.

"Even so, the scheme didn't work. The Yildivans hadn't

really comprehended our power. How could they have? Manuel himself dropped the two Lugals who were killing me. He needed exactly two shots for that. Our boys swept a ring of fire, and the enemy melted away.

"But they'd hurt us badly. When I came to, I was in the *Miriam's* sick bay. Manuel hovered over me like an anxious raven. 'How'd we do?' I think I said.

" 'You should rest, *señor*,' he said, 'and God forgive me that I made the doctor rouse you with drugs. But we must have your decision quickly. Several men are wounded. Two are dead. Three are missing. The enemy is back in the wilderness, I believe with prisoners.'

"He lifted me into a carrier and took me outside. I felt no physical pain, but was lightheaded and half crazy. You know how it is when you're filled to the cap with stimulol. Manuel told me straight out that my legbone was pretty well pulverized, but that didn't seem to matter at the time . . . What do I mean, 'seem'? Of course it didn't! Gower and Muramoto were dead. Bullis, Cheng, and Zerkowsky were gone.

"The camp was unnaturally quiet under the orange sun. My men had policed the grounds while I was unconscious. Enemy corpses were laid out in a row. Twenty-three Yildivans—that number's going to haunt me for the rest of my life—and I'm not sure how many Lugals, a hundred perhaps. I had Manuel push me along while I peered into face after still, bloody face. But I didn't recognize any.

"Our own prisoners were packed together in our main basement excavation. A couple of hundred Lugals, but only two wounded Yildivans. The rest who were hurt had been carried off by their friends. With so much construction and big machines standing around for cover, that hadn't been too hard to do. Manuel explained that he'd stopped the attack of the hostages with stunbeams. Much the best weapon. You can't prevent a Lugal fighting for his master with a mere threat to kill him.

"In a corner of the pit, glaring up at the armed men above, were the Yildivans. One I didn't know. He had a

nasty blaster burn, and our medics had give nhim seda-
tion after patching it, so he was pretty much out of the
picture anyway. But I recognized the other, who was in-
tact. A stunbeam had taken him. It was Kochihir, an adult
son of Shivaru, who'd visited us like his father a time or
two.

"We stared at each other for a space, he and I. Finally,
'Why?' I asked him. 'Why have you done this?' Each word
puffed white out of my mouth and the wind shredded it.

" 'Because they are traitors, murderers, and thieves by
nature, that's why,' Yuschenkoff said, also in Ulash. Brander's team had naturally been careful to find out whether
there were words corresponding to concepts of honor
and the reverse. I don't imagine the League will ever forget
the Darborian Semantics!

"Yuschenkoff spat at Kochihir. 'Now we shall hunt down
your breed like the animals they are,' he said. Gower had
been his brother-in-law.

" 'No,' I said at once, in Ulash, because such a growl
had risen from the Lugals that any insane thing might
have happened next. 'Speak thus no more.' Yuschenkoff
shut his mouth, and a kind of ripple went among those
packed, hairy bodies, like wind dying out on an ocean.
'But Kochihir,' I said, 'your father was my good friend. Or
so I believed. In what wise have we offended him and his
people?'

"He raised his ruff, the tail lashed his ankles, and he
snarled, 'You must go and never come back. Else we shall
harry you in the forests, roll the hillsides down on you,
stampede horned beasts through your camps, poison the
wells, and burn the grass about your feet. Go, and do not
dare return!'

"My own temper flared—which made my head spin and
throb, as if with fever—and I said, 'We shall certainly not
go unless our captive friends are returned to us. There are
drums in camp that your father gave me before he
betrayed us. Call your folk on those, Kochihir, and tell

them to bring back our folk.' After that, perhaps we can talk. Never before.'

"He fleered at me without replying.

"I beckoned to Manuel. 'No sense in stalling unnecessarily,' I said. 'We'll organize a tight defense here. Won't get taken by surprise twice. But we've got to rescue those men. Send flitters aloft to search for them. The war party can't have gone far.'

"You can best tell how you argued with me, Manuel. You said an airflit was an utter waste of energy which was badly needed elsewhere. Didn't you?"

The Nuevo Méxican looked embarrassed. "I did not wish to contradict my captain," he said. His oddly delicate fingers twisted together in his lap as he stared out into the night that had fallen. "But, indeed, I thought that aerial scouts would never find anyone in so many, many hectares of hill and ravine, water and woods. They could have dispersed, those devils. Surely, even if they traveled away in company, they would not be in such a clump that infrared detectors could see them through the forest roof. Yet I did not like to contradict my captain."

"Oh, you did, you," Per said. A corner of his mouth bent upward. "I was quite daft by then. Shouted and stormed at you, eh? Told you to jolly well obey orders and get those flitters in motion. You saluted and started off, and I called you back. You mustn't go in person. Too damned valuable here. Yes, that meant I was keeping back the one man with enough wilderness experience that he might have stood a chance of identifying spoor, even from above. But my brain was spinning down and down the sides of a maelstrom. 'See what you can do to make this furry bastard cooperate,' I said."

"It pained me a little that my captain should appoint me his torturer," Manuel confessed mildly. "Although from time to time, on various planets, when there was great need—No matter."

"I'd some notion of breaking down morale among our prisoners," Per said. "In retrospect, I see that it wouldn't

have made any difference if they had cooperated, at least
to the extent of drumming for us. The Cainites don't have
our kind of group solidarity. If Kochihir and his buddy
came to grief at our hands, that was their hard luck. But
Shivaru and some of the others had read our psychology
shrewdly enough to know what a hold on us their three
prisoners gave.

"I looked down at Kochihir. His teeth gleamed back. He
hadn't missed a syllable or a gesture, and even if he
didn't know any Anglic, he must have understood almost
exactly what was going on. By now I was slurring my
words as if drunk. So, also like a drunk, I picked them with
uncommon care. 'Kochihir,' I said, 'I have commanded
our fliers out to hunt down your people and fetch our own
whom they have captured. Can a Yildivan outrun a flying
machine? Can he fight when its guns flame at him from
above? Can he hide from its eyes that see from end to end
to horizon? Your kinfolk will dearly pay if they do not
return our men of their own accord. Take the drums,
Kochihir, and tell them so. If you do not, it will cost *you*
dearly. I have commanded my man here to do whatever
may be needful to break your will.'

"Oh, that was a vicious speech. But Gower and Muramoto had been my friends. Bullis, Cheng, and Zerkowsky
still were, if they lived. And I was on the point of passing
out. I did, actually, on the way back to the ship. I heard
Doc Leblanc mutter something about how could he be expected to treat a patient whose system was abused with
enough drugs to bloat a camel, and then the words kind
of trailed off in a long gibber that went on and on, rising
and falling until I thought I'd been turned into an elec-
tron and was trapped in an oscilloscope . . . and the darkness turned green and . . . and they tell me I was unconscious for fifty hours.

"From there on it's Manuel's story."

At this stage, Per was croaking. As he sank back in his
lounger, I saw how white he had become. One hand picked

at his blanket, and the vermouth slopped when he raised
his glass. Harry watched him, with a helpless anger that
smoldered at Van Rijn. The merchant said, "There, there,
so soon after his operation and I make him lecture us, ha?
But shortly comes dinner, no better medicine than a real
rijstaffel, and so soon after that he can walk about, he
comes to my place in Djakarta for a nice old-fashioned
orgy."

"Oh, hellfire!" Per exploded in a whisper. "Why're you
trying to make me feel good? I ruined the whole show!"

"Whoa, son," I ventured to suggest. "You were in good
spirits half an hour ago, and half an hour from now
you'll be the same. It's only that reliving the bad moments
is more punishment than Jehovah would inflict. I've been
there too." Blindly, the blue gaze sought mine. "Look,
Per," I said, "if Freeman Van Rijn thought you'd botched
a mission through your own fault, you wouldn't be lapping
his booze tonight. You'd be selling meat to the cannibals."

A ghost of a grin rewarded me.

"Well, Don Manuel," Van Rijn said, "now we hear from
you, *nie?*"

"By your favor, *señor,* I am no Don," the Nuevo Méxican said, courteously, academically, and not the least hum-
bly. "My father was a huntsman in the Sierra de los Bos-
ques Secos, and I traveled in space as a mercenary with
Rogers' Rovers, becoming sergeant before I left them for
your service. No more." He hesitated. "Nor is there much
I can relate of the happenings on Cain."

"Don't make foolishness," Van Rijn said, finished his
third or fourth liter of beer since I arrived, and signaled
for more. My own glass had been kept filled too, so much
so that the stars and the city lights had begun to dance in
the dark outside. I stuffed my pipe to help me ease off. "I
have read the official reports from your expeditioning,"
Van Rijn continued. "They are scum-dreary. I need details—the little things nobody thinks to record, like Per
has used up his lawrence in telling—I need to make a
planet real for me before this cracked old pot of mine can

maybe find a pattern. For it is my experience of many other planets, where I, even I, Nicholas van Rijn, got my nose rubbed in the dirt—which, ho, ho! takes a lot of dirt—it is on that I draw. Evolutions have parallels, but also skews, like somebody said tonight. Which lines is Cain's evolution parallel to? Talk, Ensign Gomez y Palomares. Brag. Pop jokes, sing songs, balance a chair on your head if you want—but talk!"

The brown man sat still a minute. His eyes were steady on us, save when they moved to Per and back.

"As the *señor* wishes," he began. Throughout, his tone was level, but the accent could not help singing.

"When they bore my captain away I stood in thought, until Igor Yuschenkoff said, 'Well, who is to take the flitters?'

" 'None,' I said.

" 'But we have orders,' he said.

" 'The captain was hurt and shaken. We should not have roused him,' I answered, and asked of the men who stood near, 'Is this not so?'

"They agreed, after small argument. I leaned over the edge of the pit and asked Kochihir if he would beat the drums for us. 'No,' he said, 'whatever you do.'

" 'I shall do nothing, yet,' I said. 'We will bring you food presently.' And that was done. For the rest of the short day I wandered about among the snows that lay in patches on the grass. Ay, this was a stark land, where it swooped down into the valley and then rose again at the end of sight in saw-toothed purple ranges. I thought of home and of one Dolores whom I had known, a long time ago. The men did no work; they huddled over their weapons, saying little, and toward evening the breath began to freeze on their parka hoods.

"One by one I spoke to them and chose them for those tasks I had in mind. They were all good men of their hands, but few had been hunters save in sport. I myself could not trail the Cainites far, because they had crossed a broad reach of naked rock on their way downward and once in the forest had covered their tracks. But Hamud ibn Rashid and Jacques Ngolo had been woodsmen in their day. We prepared what we needed. Then I entered the ship and looked on my captain—how still he lay!

"I ate lightly and slept briefly. Darkness had fallen when I returned to the pit. The four men we had on guard stood like deeper shadows against the stars which crowd that sky. 'Go now,' I said, and took out my own blaster. Their footfalls crunched away.

"The shapes that clotted the blackness of the pit stirred and mumbled. A voice hissed upward, 'Ohé, you are back. To torment me?' Those Cainites have eyes that see in the night like owls. I had thought, before, that they snickered within themselves when they watched us blunder about after sunset.

" 'No,' I said, 'I am only taking my turn to guard you.'

" 'You alone?' he scoffed.

" 'And this.' I slapped the blaster against my thigh.

"He fell silent. The cold gnawed deeper into me. I do not think the Cainites felt it much. As the stars wheeled slowly overhead, I began to despair of my plan. Whispers went among the captives, but otherwise I stood in a world where sound was frozen dead.

"When the thing happened, it went with devil's haste. The Lugals had been shifting about a while, as if restless. Suddenly they were upon me. One had stood on another's shoulders and leaped. To death, as they thought—but my shot missed, a quick flare and an amazed gasp from him that he was still alive. Had I not missed, several would have died to bring me down.

"As it was, two fell upon me. I went under, breaking hands loose from my throat with a judo release but held writhing by their mass. Hard fists beat me on head and belly. A palm over my mouth muffled my yells. Meanwhile the prisoners helped themselves out and fled.

"Finally I worked a leg free and gave one of them my knee. He rolled off with pain rattling in his throat. I twisted about on top of the other and struck him below the skull with the blade of my hand. When he went limp, I sprang up and shouted.

"Siren and floodlights came to life. The men swarmed from ship and tents. 'Back!' I cried. 'Not into the dark!' Many Lugals had not yet escaped, and those retreated snarling to the far side of the pit as our troop arrived. With their bodies they covered the wounded Yildivan from the guns. But we only fired, futilely, after those who were gone from sight.

"Guards posted themselves around the cellar. I scrabbled over the earth, seeking my blaster. It was gone. Someone had snatched it up: if not Kochihir, then a Lugal who would soon give it to him. Jacques Ngolo came to me and saw. 'This is bad,' he said.

" 'An evil turn of luck,' I admitted, 'but we must proceed anyhow.' I rose and stripped off my parka. Below were the helmet and spacesuit torso which had protected me in the fight. I threw them down, for they would only hinder me now, and put the parka back on. Hamud ibn Rashid joined us. He had my pack and gear and another blaster for me. I took them, and we three started our pursuit.

"By the mercy of God, we had never found occasion to demonstrate night-seeing goggles here. They made the world clear, though with a sheen over it like dreams. Ngolo's infrared tracker was our compass, the needle trembling toward the mass of Cainites that loped ahead of us. We saw them for a while, too, as they crossed the bare hillside, in and out among tumbled boulders; but we kept ourselves low lest they see us against the sky. The grass was rough in my face when I went all-fours, and the earth sucked heat out through boots and gloves. Somewhere a hunter beast screamed.

"We were panting by the time we reached the edge of trees. Yet in under their shadows we must go, before the Cainites fled farther than the compass would reach. Already it flickered, with so many dark trunks and so much brake to screen off radiation. But thus far the enemy had not stopped to hide his trail. I moved through the underbrush more carefully than him—legs brought forward to part the stems that my hands then guided to either side of my body—reading the book of trampled bush and snapped branch.

"After an hour we were well down in the valley. Tall trees gloomed everywhere about; the sky was hidden, and I must tune up the photomultiplier unit in my goggles. Now the book began to close. The Cainites were moving at a natural pace, confident of their escape, and even without special effort they left little spoor. And since they were now less frantic and more alert, we must follow so far behind that infrared detection was of no further use.

"At last we came to a meadow, whose beaten grass showed that they had paused here a while. And that was seen which I feared. The party had broken into three or four, each bound a different way. 'Which do we choose?' Ngolo asked.

" 'Three of us can follow three of them,' I said.

" '*Bismillah!*' Hamud grunted. 'Blaster or no, I would not care to face such a band alone. But what must be, must be.'

"We took so much time to ponder what clues the forest gave that the east was gray before we parted. Plainly, the Lugals had gone toward their masters' homes, while Kochihir's own slaves had accompanied him. And Kochihir was the one we desired. I could only guess that the largest party was his, because most likely the first break had been made under his orders by his own Lugals, whose capabilities he knew. That path I chose for myself. Hamud and Ngolo wanted it too, but I used my rank to seize the honor, that folk on Nuevo México might never say a Gomez lacked courage.

"So great a distance was now between that there was no reason not to use our radios to talk with each other and with the men in camp. That was often consoling, in the long time which was upon me. For it was slow, slow, tracing those woods-wily hunters through their own land. I do not believe I could have done it, had they been only Yildivans and such Lugals as are regularly used in the chase. But plain to see, the attack had been strengthened by calling other Lugals from fields and mines and household tasks, and those were less adept.

"Late in the morning, Ngolo called. 'My gang just reached a cave and a set of lean-tos,' he said. 'I sit in a tree and watch them met by some female and half-grown Yildivans. They shuffle off to their own shed. This is where they belong, I suppose, and they are not going farther. Shall I return to the meadow and pick up another trail?'

" 'No,' I said, 'it would be too cold by now. Backtrack to a spot out of view and have a flitter fetch you.'

"Some hours later, the heart leaped in my breast. For I came upon a tree charred by unmistakable blaster shots. Kochihir had been practicing.

"I called Hamud and asked where he was. 'On the bank of a river,' he said, 'casting about the place where they crossed. That was a bitter stream to wade!'

" 'Go no farther,' I said. 'My path is the right one. Have yourself taken back to camp.'

" 'What?' he asked. 'Shall we not join you now?'

" 'No,' I said. 'It is uncertain how near I am to the end. Perhaps so near that a flitter would be seen by them as it came down and alarm them. Stand by.' I confess it was a lonely order to give.

"A few times I stopped to eat and rest. But stimulants kept me going in a way that would have surprised my quarry who despised me. By evening his trail was again so fresh that I slacked my pace and went on with a snake's caution. Down here, after sunset, the air was not so cold as on the heights; yet every leaf glistened hoar in what starlight pierced through.

"Not much into the night, my own infrared detector began to register a source, stronger than living bodies could account for. I whispered the news into my radio and then ordered no more communication until further notice, lest we be overheard. Onward I slipped. The forest rustled and creaked about me, somewhere far off a heavy animal broke brush in panic flight, wings whirred overhead, yet *Santa María,* how silent and alone it was!

"Until I came to the edge of a small clearing.

"A fire burned there, throwing unrestful shadows on the wall of a big, windowless log cabin which nestled under the trees beyond. Two Yildivans leaned on their spears. And light glimmered from the smoke hole in the roof.

"Most softly, I drew my stun gun. The bolt snicked twice, and they fell in heaps. At once I sped across the open ground, crouched in the shadow under that rough wall, and waited.

"But no one had heard. I glided to the doorway. Only a leather curtain blocked my view. I twitched it aside barely enough that I might peer within.

"The view was dimmed by smoke, but I could see that there was just one long room. It did not seem plain, so beautiful were the furs hung and draped everywhere about. A score or so of Yildivans, mostly grown males, squatted in a circle around the fire, which burned in a pit and picked their fierce flat countenances out of the dark. Also there were several Lugals hunched in a corner. I recognized old Cherkez among them, and was glad he had outlived the battle. The Lugals in Kochihir's party must have been sent to barracks. He himself was telling his father Shivaru of his escape.

"As yet the time was unripe for happiness, but I vowed to light many candles for the saints. Because this was as I had hoped: Kochihir had not gone to his own home, but sought an agreed rendezvous. Zerkowsky, Cheng, and Bullis were here. They sat in another corner at the far end of the room, coughing from the smoke, skins drawn around them to ward off the cold.

"Kochihir finished his account and looked at his father for approval. Shivaru's tail switched back and forth. 'Strange that they were so careless about you,' he said.

" 'They are like blind cubs,' Kochihir scoffed.

" 'I am not so sure,' the old Yildivan murmured. 'Great are their powers. And . . . we know what they did in the past." Then suddenly he grew stiff, and his whisper struck out like a knife. 'Or did they do it? Tell me again, Kochihir, how the master ordered one thing and the rest did another.'

" 'No, now, that means nothing,' said a different Yildivan, scarred and grizzled. 'What we must devise is a use for these captives. You have thought they might trade our Lugals and Gumush, whom Kochihir says they still hold, for three of their own. But I say, Why should they? Let us instead place the bodies where the *Erziran* can find them, in such condition that they will be warned away.'

" 'Just so,' said Bokzahan, whom I now spied in the gloom. 'Tulitur and I proved they are weak and foolish.'

" 'First we should try to bargain,' said Shivaru. 'If that fails . . .' His fangs gleamed in the firelight.

" 'Make an example of one, then, before we talk,' Kochihir said angrily. 'They threatened the same for me.'

"A rumble went among them, as from a beast's cage in the zoo. I thought with terror of what might be done. For my captain has told you how no Yildivan is in authority over any other. Whatever his wishes, Shivaru could not stop them from doing what they would.

"I must decide my own course immediately. Blaster bolts could not destroy them all fast enough to keep them from hurling the weapons that lay to hand upon me—not unless I set the beam so wide that our men must also be killed. The stun gun was better, yet it would not overpower them either before I went down under axes and clubs. By standing to one side I could pen them within, for they had only the single door. But Bullis, Cheng, and Zerkowsky would remain hostages.

"What I did was doubtless stupid, for I am not my captain. I sneaked back to the edge of the woods and called the men in camp. 'Come as fast as may be,' I said, and left the radio going for them to home on. Then I circled about and found a tree overhanging the cabin. Up I went, and down again from a branch to the sod roof, and so to the smoke hole. Goggles protected my eyes, but nostrils withered in the fumes that poured forth. I filled my lungs with clean air and leaned forward to see.

"Best would have been if they had gone to bed. Then I could have stunned them one by one as they slept, without risk. But they continued to sit about and quarrel over what to do with their captives. How hard those poor men tried to be brave, as that dreadful snarling broke around them, as slit eyes turned their way and hands went stroking across knives!

"The time felt long, but I had not completed the Rosary in my mind when thunder awoke. Our flitters came down the sky like hawks. The Yildivans roared. Two or three of them dashed out the door to see what was afoot. I dropped them with my stunner, but not before one had screamed, 'The *Erziran* are here!'

"My face went back to the smoke hole. It was turmoil below. Kochihir screeched and pulled out his blaster. I fired but missed. Too many bodies in between, *señores*. There is no other excuse for me.

"I took the gun in my teeth, seized the edge of the smoke hole, and swung myself as best I could before letting go. Thus I struck the dirt floor barely outside the firepit, rolled over and bounced erect. Cherkez leaped for my throat. I sent him reeling with a kick to the belly, took my gun, and fired around me.

"Kochihir could not be seen in the mob which struggled from wall to wall. I fought my way toward the prisoners. Shivaru's ax whistled down. By the grace of God, I dodged it, twisted about and stunned him point-blank. I squirmed between two others. A third got on my back. I snapped my head against his mouth and felt flesh give way. He let go. With my gun arm and my free hand I tossed a Lugal aside and saw Kochihir. He had reached the men. They shrank from him, too stupefied to fight. Hate was on his face, in his whole body, as he took unpracticed aim.

"He saw me at his sight's edge and spun. The blaster crashed, blinding in that murk. But I had dropped to one knee as I pulled trigger. The beam scorched my parka hood. He toppled. I pounced, got the blaster, and whirled to stand before our people.

"Bokzahan raised his ax and threw it. I blasted it in mid air and then killed him. Otherwise I used the stunner. And in a minute or two more, the matter was finished. A grenade brought down the front wall of the cabin. The Cainites fell before a barrage of knockout beams. We left them to awaken and returned to camp."

Again silence grew upon us. Manuel asked if he might smoke, politely declined Van Rijn's cigars, and took a vicious-looking brown cigarette from his own case. That was a lovely, grotesque thing, wrought in silver on some planet I could not identify.

"Whoof!" Van Rijn gusted. "But this is not the whole story, from what you have written. They came to see you before you left."

Per nodded. "Yes, sir," he said. A measure of strength had rearisen in him. "We'd about finished our preparations when Shivaru himself arrived, with ten other Yildivans and their Lugals. They walked slowly into the compound, ruffs erect and tails held stiff, looking neither to right nor left. I guess they wouldn't have been surprised to be shot down. I ordered such of the boys as were covering them to holster guns and went out on my carrier to say hello with due formality.

"Shivaru responded just as gravely. Then he got almost tongue-tied. He couldn't really apologize. Ulash doesn't have the phrases for it. He beckoned to Cherkez. 'You were good to release our people whom you held,' he said." Per chuckled. "Huh! What else were we supposed to do, keep feeding them? Cherkez gave him a leather bag. 'I bring a gift,' he told me, and pulled out Tulitur's head. 'We shall return as much of the goods he got from you as we can find,' he promised, 'and if you will give us time, we shall bring double payment for everything else.'

"I'm afraid that after so much blood had gone over the dam, I didn't find the present as gruesome as I ought. I only sputtered that we didn't require such tokens.

" 'But we do,' he said, 'to cleanse our honor.'

"I invited them to eat, but they declined. Shivaru made haste to explain that they didn't feel right about accepting our hospitality until their debt was paid off. I told them we were pulling out. Though that was obvious from the state of the camp, they still looked rather dismayed. So I told them we, or others like us, would be back, but first it was necessary to get our injured people home.

"Another mistake of mine. Because being reminded of what they'd done to us upset them so badly that they only mumbled when I tried to find out why they'd done it. I decided best not press that issue—the situation being delicate yet—and they left with relief branded on them.

"We should have stuck around a while, maybe, because we've got to know what the trouble was before committing more men and equipment to Cain. Else it's all too likely to flare up afresh. But between our being shorthanded, and having a couple of chaps who needed first-class medical treatment, I didn't think we could linger. All the way home we wondered and argued. What had gone wrong? And what, later, had gone right? We still don't know."

Van Rijn's eyes glittered at him. "What is your theory?" he demanded.

"Oh—" Per spread his hands. "Yuschenkoff's, more or less. They were afraid we were the spearhead of an invasion. When we acted reasonably decently—refraining from mistreatment of prisoners, thanks to Manuel, and using stunners rather than blasters in the rescue operation—they decided they were mistaken."

Manuel had not shifted a muscle in face or body, as far as I could see. But Van Rijn's battleship prow of a nose swung toward him and the merchant laughed, "You have maybe a little different notion, ha? Come, spew it out."

"My place is not to contradict my captain," said the Nuevo Méxican.

"So why you make fumblydiddles against orders, that day on Cain? When you know better, then you got a duty, by damn, to tell us where to stuff our heads."

"If the *señor* commands. But I am no learned man. I have no book knowledge of studies made on the psychonomy. It is only that . . . that I think I know those Yildivans. They seem not so unlike men of the barranca country on my home world, and again among the Rovers."

"How so?"

"They live very near death, their whole lives. Courage and skill in fighting, those are what they most need to survive, and so are what they most treasure. They thought, seeing us use machines and weapons that kill from afar, seeing us blinded by night and most of us clumsy in the woods, hearing us talk about what our life is like at home —they thought we lacked *cojones*. So they scorned us. They owed us nothing, since we were spiritless and could never understand their own spirit. We were only fit to be the prey, first of their wits and then of their weapons." Manuel's shoulders drew straight. His voice belled out so that I jumped in my seat. "When they found how terrible men are, that they themselves are the weak ones, we changed in their eyes from peasants to kings!"

Van Rijn sucked noisily on his cigar. "Any other shipboard notions?" he asked.

"No, sir, those were our two schools of thought," Per said.

Van Rijn guffawed. "So! Take comfort, freemen. No need for angelometrics on pinheads. Relax and drink. You are both wrong."

"I *beg* your pardon," Harry rapped. "You were not there, may I say."

"No, not in the flesh." Van Rijn slapped his paunch. "Too much flesh for that. But tonight I have been on Cain up here, in this old brain, and it is rusty and afloat in alcohol but it has stored away more information about the universe than maybe the universe gets credit for holding. I see now what the parallels are. Xanadu, Dunbar, Tametha, Disaster Landing . . . oh, the analogue is never exact and on Cain the thing I am thinking of has gone far and far . . . but still I see the pattern, and what happened makes sense.

"Not that we have got to have an analogue. You gave us so many clues here that I could solve the puzzle by logic alone. But analogues help, and also they show my conclusion is not only correct but possible."

Van Rijn paused. He was so blatantly waiting to be coaxed that Harry and I made a long performance out of refreshing our drinks. Van Rijn turned purple, wheezed a while, decided to keep his temper for a better occasion, and chortled.

"Hokay, you win," he said. "I tell you short and fast, because very soon we eat if the cook has not fallen in the curry. Later you can study the formal psychologics.

"The key to this problem is the Lugals. You have been calling them slaves, and there is your mistake. They are not. They are domestic animals."

Per sat bolt upright. "Can't be!" he exclaimed. "Sir. I mean, they have language and—"

"*Ja, ja, ja,* for all I care they do mattress algebra in their heads. They are still tame animals. What is a slave, anyhows? A man who has got to do what another man says, willy-billy. Right? Harry said he would not trust a slave with weapons, and I would not either, because history is too pocked up with slave revolts and slaves running away and slaves dragging their feet and every such foolishness. But your big fierce expensive dogs, Harry, you trust them with their teeth, *nie?* When your kids was little and wet, you left them alone in rooms with a dog to keep watches. There is the difference. A slave may or not obey. But a domestic animal has got to obey. His genes won't let him do anything different.

"Well, you yourselves figured the Yildivans had kept

Lugals so long, breeding them for what traits they wanted, that this had changed the Lugal nature. Must be so. Otherwise the Lugals would be slaves, not animals, and could not always be trusted the way you saw they were. You also guessed the Yildivans themselves must have been affected, and this is very sleek thinking only you did not carry it so far you ought. Because everything you tell about the Yildivans goes to prove by nature they are *wild* animals.

"I mean wild, like tigers and buffalos. They have no genes for obediences, except to their parents when they are little. So long have they kept Lugals to do the dirty work—before they really became intelligent, I bet, like ants keeping aphids; for remember, you found no Lugals that was not kept—any gregarious-making genes in the Yildivans, any inborn will to be led, has gone foof. This must be so. Otherwise, from normal variation in ability, some form of Yildivan ranks would come to exist, *nie?*

"This pops your fear-of-invasion theory, Per Stenvik. With no concept of a tribe or army, they can't have any notions about conquest. And wild animals don't turn humble when they are beat, Manuel Gomez y Palomares, the way you imagine. A man with a superiority complexion may lick your boots when you prove you are his better; but an untamed carnivore hasn't got any such pride in the first place. He is plain and simple independent of you.

"Well, then, what did actual go on in their heads?

"Recapitalize. Humans land and settle down to deal. Yildivans have no experience of races outside their own planet. They natural assume you think like them. In puncture of fact, I believe they could not possible imagine anything else, even if they was told. Your findings about their culture structure shows their half-symbiosis with the Lugals is psychological too; they are specialized in the brains, not near so complicated as man.

"But as they get better acquaintanced, what do they see? People taking orders. How can this be? No Yildivan ever took orders, unless to save his life when an enemy stood over him with a sharp thing. Ah, ha! So some of the strangers is Lugal type. Pretty soon, I bet, old Shivaru decides all of you is Lugal except young Stenvik, because in the end all orders come from him. Some others, like Manuel, is straw bosses maybe, but no more. Tame animals.

"And then Per mentions the idea of God."

Van Rijn crossed himself with a somewhat irritating piety. "I make no blasfuming," he said. "But everybody knows our picture of God comes in part from our kings. If you want to know how Oriental kings in ancient days was spoken to, look in your prayer book. Even now, we admit He is the Lord, and we is supposed to do His will, hoping He will not take too serious a few things that happen to anybody like anger, pride, envy, gluttony, lust, sloth, greed, and the rest what makes life fun.

"Per said this. So Per admitted he had a master. But then he must also be a Lugal—an animal. No Yildivan could possible confess to having even a mythical master, as shown by the fact they have no religion themselves though their Lugals seem to.

"Give old boy Shivaru his credits, he came again with some friends to ask further. What did he learn? He already knew everybody else was a Lugal, because of obeying. Now Per said he was no better than the rest. This confirmed Per was also a Lugal. And what blew the cork out of the bottle was when Per said he nor none of them had any owners at home!

"Whup, whup, slow down, youngster. You could not have known. Always we make discoveries the hard way. Like those poor Yildivans.

"They was real worried, you can imagine. Even dogs turn on people now and then, and surely some Lugals go bad once in a while on Cain and make big trouble before they can get killed. The Yildivans had seen some of your powers, knew you was dangerous . . . and your breed of Lugal must have gone mad and killed off its own Yildivans. How else could you be Lugals and yet have no masters?

"So. What would you and I do, friends, if we lived in lonely country houses and a pack of wild dogs what had killed people set up shop in our neighborhood?"

Van Rijn gurgled beer down his throat. We pondered for a while. "Seems pretty farfetched," Harry said.

"No." Per's cheeks burned with excitement. "It fits. Freeman Van Rijn put into words what I always felt as I got to know Shivaru. A—a single-mindedness about him. As if he was incapable of seeing certain things, grasping certain ideas, though his reasoning faculties were intrinsically as good as mine. Yes . . ."

I nodded at my pipe, which had been with me when I clashed against stranger beings than that.

"So two of them first took advantage of you," Van Rijn said, "to swindle away what they could before the attack because they wasn't sure the attack would work. No shame there. You was outside the honor concept, being animals. Animals whose ancestors must have murdered a whole race of true humans, in their views. Then the alarmed males tried to scrub you out. They failed, but hoped maybe to use their prisoners for a lever to pry you off their country. Only Manuel fooled them."

"But why'd they change their minds about us?" Per asked.

Van Rijn wagged his finger. "Ha, there you was lucky. You gave a very clear and important order. Your men disobeyed every bit of it. Now Lugals might go crazy and kill off Yildivans, but they are so bred to being bossed that they can't stand long against a leader. Or if they do, it's because they is too crazy to think straight. Manuel, though, was thinking straight like a plumber line. His strategy worked five-four-three-two-one-zero. Also, your people did not kill more Yildivans than was needful, which crazy Lugals would do.

"So you could not be domestic animals after all, gone bad or not. Therefore you had to be wild animals. The

Cainite mind—a narrow mind like you said—can't imagine any third horn on that special bull. If you had proved you was not Lugal type, you must be Yildivan type. Indications to the contrariwise, the way you seemed to take orders or acknowledge a Lord, those must have been misunderstandings on the Cainites' part.

"Once he had time to reason this out, Shivaru saw his people had done yours dirty. Partway he felt bad about it in his soul, if he has one stowed somewhere; Yildivans do have some notion about upright behavior to other Yildivans. And besides, he did not want to lose a chance at your fine trade goods. He convinced his friends. They did what best they could think about to make amendments."

Van Rijn rubbed his palms together in glee. "Oh, ho, ho, what customers they will be for us!" he roared.

We sat still for another time, digesting the idea, until the butler announced dinner. Manuel helped Per rise. "We'll have to instruct everybody who goes to Cain," the young man said. "I mean, not to let on that we aren't wild animals, we humans."

"But, Captain," Manuel said, and his head lifted high, "we are."

Van Rijn stopped and looked at us a while. Then he shook his own head violently and shambled bearlike to the viewer wall. "No," he growled. "Some of us are."

"How's that?" Harry wondered.

"We here in this room are wild," Van Rijn said. "We do what we do because we want to or because it is right. No other motivations, *nie?* If you made slaves of us, you would for sure not be wise to let us near a weapon.

"But how many slaves has there been, in Earth's long history, that their masters could trust? Quite some! There was even armies of slaves, like the Janissaries. And how many people today is domestic animals at heart? Wanting somebody else should tell them what to do, and take care of their needfuls, and protect them not just against their fellow men but against themselves? Why has every free human society been so short-lived? Is this not because the wild-animal men are born so heartbreaking seldom?"

He glared out across the city, where it winked and glittered beneath the stars, around the curve of the planet. "Do you think they yonder is free?" he shouted. His hand chopped downward in scorn.

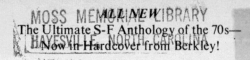

ALL NEW
The Ultimate S-F Anthology of the 70s—
Now in Hardcover from Berkley!

EPOCH

24 never-before-published masterworks of science fiction—edited by Roger Elwood and Robert Silverberg and including:

A complete novel by JACK VANCE

Novellas by LARRY NIVEN—ALEXEI and CORY PANSHIN—A.A. ATTANASIO

Novelettes by CLIFFORD SIMAK—BRIAN ALDISS—HARRY HARRISON—GORDON ECKLUND

Stories by URSULA Le GUIN—R.A. LAFFERTY—KATE WILHELM—FREDERIK POHL—BARRY MALZBERG

and much, much more!

Keep in touch with the state of the art today—don't miss EPOCH!

623 pages $10.95

Send for a *free* list of all our books in print

These books are available at your local bookstore, or send price indicated plus 30¢ per copy to cover mailing costs to

Berkley Publishing Corporation
200 Madison Avenue
New York, New York 10016